"Sam?" Lizzie ran into the bathroom.

Sam was stuck in a hole in the floor. "I've fallen through your rotting sixteenth-century floor. Don't come any closer or we could both go through."

"Are you sure you're not hurt?" He was naked. Gloriously naked, from what she could see. His hair was wet, dripping onto those incredible shoulders. He had that broad, bare back to her, so she didn't feel quite so awkward approaching him. Backs were a lot safer to look at than fronts.

"I don't think so, but something is digging into my…thigh and I don't want to make any sudden moves, if you know what I mean."

She knew what he meant. She got down on her hands and knees and crawled closer. "Let me see."

"No way."

"I'm not going to be overcome with lust at the sight of a naked man."

"I'm not talking about lust. This morning you were threatening mutilation. I'm not taking any chances."

"I was married once," she reminded him. "Isn't the expression, 'If you've seen one you've seen them all'?"

He opened his mouth and, as if changing his mind about responding, closed it again. "You're not seeing this one, lady. The last time we talked you threatened to unman me." He looked down at the place where his thighs were encased in flooring. "Looks like this damn house has done it for you."

Dear Reader,

Our Let's Celebrate! promotion is coming to an end this month, so take advantage of your last chance to enter our sweepstakes. A fabulous collection of romantic comedy videos is the prize.

Carrie Alexander, a RITA nominee, continues the adventures of the peculiar but fascinating Fairchild family from *The Madcap Heiress* with Augustina Fairchild's story. *The Amorous Heiress* is a truly delightful romp.

Longtime and incredibly successful romance author Kristine Rolofson joins our Matchmaking Mothers (from Hell) lineup with *Pillow Talk*. As a mother of six who has also published over twenty books, Kristine is obviously a woman who is able to balance a busy career and family life very well. (Perhaps with a lot of love and laughter?) She certainly handled the matchmaking mother concept with ease. We can't help but wonder if her own children are getting a little nervous?

Wishing you another month filled with much love and laughter,

Malle Vallik

Malle Vallik
Associate Senior Editor

PILLOW TALK

Kristine Rolofson

Harlequin Books

TORONTO • NEW YORK • LONDON
AMSTERDAM • PARIS • SYDNEY • HAMBURG
STOCKHOLM • ATHENS • TOKYO • MILAN
MADRID • WARSAW • BUDAPEST • AUCKLAND

ISBN 0-373-44027-8

PILLOW TALK

Kristine Rolofson is one busy and amazing lady. The author of over twenty books, all published by Harlequin, she is also a mother of six! A Rhode Island native, she now resides in the same town where she spent her childhood. Writing about family life is one of the strong themes in her books. *Romantic Times* gave *The Texan Takes a Wife* a 4¹/₂ Gold Star (their very highest rating) and had this to say: "Jam-packed with vividly appealing characters, this romantic romp captivates our hearts and delivers extraordinary reading bliss." Known for her light, humorous style, Kristine is a wonderful addition to the Love & Laughter lineup!

Books by Kristine Rolofson

HARLEQUIN TEMPTATION
507—PLAIN JANE'S MAN
548—JESSIE'S LAWMAN
604—THE TEXAN TAKES A WIFE
617—THE LAST MAN IN MONTANA (Boots & Booties)
621—THE ONLY MAN IN WYOMING (Boots & Booties)
625—THE NEXT MAN IN TEXAS (Boots & Booties)
653—THE BRIDE RODE WEST

Don't miss any of our special offers. Write to us at the following address for information on our newest releases.

Harlequin Reader Service
U.S.: 3010 Walden Ave., P.O. Box 1325, Buffalo, NY 14269
Canadian: P.O. Box 609, Fort Erie, Ont. L2A 5X3

For Barbara Beshir, a dear friend and a very special lady.
You are missed by all who loved you.

1

"OUR NEXT STOP will be another one of the grand country homes in England, Longley House. The first earl of Longford was, of course, advisor to the *first* Elizabeth, Queen of England." Their tour guide, a voluptuous brunette with a dusky voice, moved the microphone away from her lips and whispered something to the bus driver.

"I knew that," Betsy whispered. "I read about Longley in *Majesty* magazine last month." She patted her son's knee. "This is so exciting."

Sam Martin wished he felt the same way. His mother's excitement never wavered, no matter how many long days they'd spent together on the bus tour, no matter how many country homes she'd explored or how many English landscapes she'd photographed. He was happy she was having a wonderful time; he simply wished he could share her enjoyment.

His response was the same one he'd given for the past five days. "I'm glad you're having a good time."

"And I'm glad you could come with me on such short notice, though I am sorry your Aunt Mary fell down those stairs," Betsy said with a sigh. "But isn't it nice that the two of us could spend time together?"

"Very nice." He looked out the window as yet another mile of English countryside rolled off to the horizon. Five days and six nights—if you counted sleeping on the plane—away from Connecticut could definitely be described as "spending time together."

"But, still, I'm glad you took a vacation, with or without me. You work too hard," his mother said for the millionth time. "It's not healthy."

"I like my work," he said. At least, he used to. Martin Construction practically ran itself. The challenge was gone. Lately he'd wondered if he was ready for a change.

She shrugged, unimpressed. "There's more to life."

"Yes, you're right." It was easier to agree than argue with her. Betsy had never been easy to argue with.

She patted his knee and gave him a sympathetic look. "I'm sorry, honey. I shouldn't nag you, not when you've been so nice to give me this retirement gift. And then you were so sweet to go along with me. I think I'm going to *love* being retired. And after you're married, think of all the time I'll have to devote myself to the grandchildren."

Her son had to smile. Despite all his attempts to convince her that he had no intention of marrying any of the women he dated, Betsy remained convinced that she would become a grandmother. And soon. In the past few years, every woman he took to dinner thought of him as a potential husband. It was that "nice guy" factor, he figured. Women looked at him and saw a healthy man with an equally healthy bank account. He was the kind of man who wouldn't beat his wife or kick the cat or protest taking his turn at driving the soccer car pool. He'd become marriage material, nothing more. Nothing less.

And he didn't like the feeling. What ever happened to passion? To love? Sam looked past his mother, out the window to where a huge stone building glowed in the afternoon sun. "There's Longley House," he said, hoping to distract her.

She turned and gazed out the window. "Oh, my, Sam. It's enormous."

Miss Dianne picked up her microphone again. "As we approach, it is certainly possible to imagine Queen Elizabeth and her court visiting great houses like these, isn't it? One of her favorite advisors was the first earl, so it is likely she visited here."

"Oh, my," Betsy said again. "Of course it is."

His mother was going to start in about Queen Elizabeth again. He could feel it.

"I've always had that affinity for Queen Elizabeth," she murmured.

We have the same birthday.

"We have the same birthday, September 7."

"That's only one week away," Sam pointed out, hoping to change the subject. "Have you thought of what you'd like as your gift this year?"

"Grandchildren."

"Other than that."

She ignored him, looking past him to the window. "The queen and I both had fathers named Henry."

And mothers named Anne.

"And mothers named Anne."

"And," he said aloud, "an older sister named Mary."

"Yes," the older woman sighed. "I'm going to be seventy-four and Mary's going to be seventy-eight. She really had no business climbing that lookout tower in Montana. Even if she did think she saw a forest fire."

"No, you're right, she didn't."

"You can't tell Mary anything. She doesn't listen to advice."

"No." It was a trait that ran in the family.

The microphone squawked as the tour guide lifted it again. Ms. Mortimer was about forty and the youngest person on the bus, aside from him. The way she held the rounded tip of the microphone and smiled at Sam made him shift in his seat. Miss Dianne, as she was known, had made her interest in an American bachelor quite clear. He'd had a hell of a time keeping her at a distance. Somehow lust and a busload of gray-haired ladies didn't mix.

Besides, he was supposed to be keeping his mother company, not "doing it" with the tour guide against the back wall of a gloomy cathedral. Miss Dianne had whispered that particular suggestion in Westminster Abbey on the second day of the trip.

"We'll be approaching Longley House in a few minutes. On your left you'll see what remains of the famous Longley Park. Descendants of the original Tudor deer herd still graze here. One of the remaining members of the Longford family, Lady Elizabeth, has devoted her life to preserving her family's ancient home. Built on the site of an abbey, Longley House was built, rebuilt and remodeled according to the whims of the various earls of Longford."

The bus swung into a wide, tree-lined area, and Miss Dianne clung to the pole to keep her balance. "We shall spend three hours here. You may tour the house and, since it's such a lovely afternoon, the grounds. For those of you who would like to use the facilities, there are toilets attached to one of the outbuildings before you approach the entrance."

She looked at her watch. "Let's plan to meet here at four. We still have a bit of a ride to our hotel tonight, where we will make our plans for the final two days of our tour together. All right?'' She smiled brightly. ''Have a lovely time, and let's all return here promptly, shall we?''

His mother was busy stuffing her purse full of necessary objects, like sunglasses, hard candies and tissues. She draped her camera strap around her neck and slapped a baseball cap on her gray curls. ''I'm ready,'' she announced, sliding off the bus seat and standing in the aisle. ''Are you?''

He was ready for a beer in a pub. He was ready for a hot shower. He was ready to get on a plane and head for home.

''Go ahead. I'm right behind you.''

''Sammy, my dear,'' another elderly lady called. ''Could you help me for just a minute?''

''Certainly, Mrs. Barrett,'' he said, recognizing the voice. He waited for the aisle to clear before moving to the seat where the lady struggled to her feet. He didn't know how she managed to see everything, but she did the best she could with feet that didn't cooperate and a sturdy cane that did.

''There,'' he said, helping her to stand and steadying her while she adjusted her purse and her cane. ''All right?''

''Just fine thank you, dear.''

Sam caught the driver's eye, and the man nodded and prepared to help the woman down the bus steps.

Miss Dianne had more sense than to nuzzle against him while his mother waited impatiently on the gravel path that led to the estate, but she winked at him as he took his mother's elbow.

She handed him two tickets for their entry to Longley. "Is there anything special you're interested in seeing at Longley, Sam?"

"Not specifically, no."

Betsy had her finger holding a page open in her *Country Estates of Britain* handbook. "I can't wait to see this house," she said. "The fortune-teller at Canterbury told me that I would meet my destiny in a gold castle with a blue bedroom."

Miss Dianne's pouty lips turned down. "Yes, I remember. You were four minutes late returning to the bus."

Betsy looked apologetic. "I apologized at least ten times for that, and there were three other people who were later than I was."

The tour guide shrugged and moved in the opposite direction. "Do be on time today, Mrs. Martin. I'm going to get a drink."

Sam ignored Miss Dianne's silent invitation and guided his mother toward the massive pile of stone that waited several hundred yards away. He made certain to walk slowly, but even Mrs. Barrett outdistanced him, and his mother grew impatient with his speed.

"Oh, do hurry, Sam," she said. "We don't have all afternoon to find the blue bedroom."

So much for trying to slow her down. Sam picked up the pace, but stopped to help Mrs. Barrett negotiate a set of wide stone steps.

"My, my," Mrs. Barrett said, gazing at the house. "Have you ever seen a house like that?"

The three of them stared at the enormous stone building. Four stories of golden stone faced them, along with an odd spiked roof and hundreds of narrow rectangular windows. It looked about as welcoming as an ancient prison, Sam thought, but the two ladies on either side of him were in raptures as they moved toward the arched doorway where the others were disappearing.

"The golden castle," Betsy repeated. "Just what the fortune-teller said."

"Is it a castle?" he had to ask.

"No. It was an ancient abbey at one time, then the Longford family owned it and built something fancier," his mother explained, opening her guidebook. "Let's see," she muttered, but Sam tapped the book shut.

"There will be detailed guidebooks inside, in the gift shop," he said, knowing that would make the ladies happy. One thing he'd learned was that there was no shortage of gift shops. They sold sweatshirts and postcards, guidebooks of all sizes and prices, ceramic miniatures of castles and houses and video-tapes of the tour, should he want to relive the trip from the comfort of his living room.

His mother had bought no fewer than seventeen miniature houses and two sweatshirts.

"I don't want to miss that bedroom," his mother muttered. "Imagine having a destiny after all these years."

"We'll see the blue bedroom. We'll see lots of bedrooms." He eyed the towering monstrosity of a house with something like despair. They entered through a stone archway and headed toward the front door. He guessed that they walked across the stone area that would have been the courtyard. "There must be fifty bedrooms in this place, and they're full of destinies." He winked at Mrs. Barrett. "There are most likely enough destinies for the three of us."

"Sammy, dear, this is no time to tease. After all, I—"

"Mother." He stopped her worrying by raising one hand. "Let's go inside for the tour."

A tall, elderly man, his hair white and his expression grim, took their tickets and handed them gold-edged leaflets titled "Life at Longley."

"It says here the tour is self-directed," Mrs. Barrett said. "We can go at our own pace."

"Does it say where the bedrooms are?"

"There's a map. Look." Mrs. Barrett showed

Betsy her unfolded brochure. "We're at the court-yard entrance, I think. If we go inside and turn left we can start the tour with the Tudor kitchen."

Sam looked at the elderly doorkeeper. "Excuse me." The man looked down at him as if he were a peasant come to deliver a wagon of wheat. "Are we in the courtyard?"

"Yes, sir. That is precisely where you are." The man turned away and picked up a notebook.

"He looks like a butler," Betsy whispered.

The man didn't turn his head as he replied. "Madam, I *am* the butler."

"Oh."

Mrs. Barrett stifled a giggle, and Sam ushered both women through the wide doorway before his mother could respond. Betsy refused to be rushed. She hesitated, saying, "Oh, I do apologize, sir," before Sam urged her forward.

"Mother," he said. "Watch out for the stairs."

"Stop fussing. I'm fine."

Sam helped Mrs. Barrett up the three wide stone steps, then let the ladies set the pace. They voted to skip the kitchen and head right to "the good stuff," as Betsy described the fancier rooms.

Three more days, Sam promised himself. He loved his mother more than he had ever loved anyone, but three more days and he could go home.

Sam could hardly wait.

"Oh, my." Betsy paused in front of a sixteenth-century painting of Queen Elizabeth. Her Majesty looked regal, her red hair glowing as bright as the jewels that covered her velvet dress. Betsy felt a little light-headed. Despite the high ceilings, the room was more than a little stuffy. Of course it would be, with all of the velvet hangings around the bed.

"The blue bedroom," Sam said, quite unnecessarily.

Grace Barrett nodded. "It is very, um, blue."

"And gold." Betsy surveyed the room, fanned herself with the Longley pamphlet and waited for her destiny to be revealed as Grace read from the pamphlet.

"The large Gobelin tapestries were purchased by the fifth earl. The painting over the fireplace is of Charles I's children, a copy after Van Dyck's original. The large cabinet opposite the sixteenth-century bed is a rare French marquetry by Pierre Gole."

The three of them stared obediently at the cabinet, an intricate and detailed piece of furniture that made Betsy long to start opening its drawers. Sam helped Grace sit in a nondescript chair by the door that was obviously meant for weary tourists.

"The blue bed looks like it's ready to fall apart," he said, coming over to stand beside her.

"It has atmosphere." Betsy felt obligated to defend the shabby bed, Lord only knew why. Its heavy silk covers were worn, its threads and holes showing. The sight saddened her, and she blinked back tears.

"'Atmosphere.' *Dust* is more like it." Sam frowned.

Her son was a sweet man, Betsy thought, but entirely too serious. Grace sneezed. The traitor.

"Bless you." Betsy fanned herself harder as she approached the bed. She got as close as she could, before those velvet ropes stopped her.

"Excuse me," her friend said. "It must be the dust."

"Or the perfume," Betsy sniffed.

"I don't smell anything."

"Perfume?" Her son stood next to her. "Mother, you're looking very pale."

"I'm fine," she insisted, stepping closer to the painting of Queen Elizabeth I. The smell grew stronger, and Betsy's ability to take air into her lungs decreased alarmingly. "Or maybe I'm not."

She felt Sam's hand on her arm as the darkness covered her sight. A buzzing in her ears was the last thing she heard before she felt her knees buckle and she collapsed into her son's arms.

ELIZABETH LOVED her "lady of the manor" outfit. Sprigged muslin and pearls went together nicely, and the long skirts hid her comfortable flat-soled shoes. If she added white gloves and a few plumes in her hair, Lizzie supposed she would be dressed well enough to have tea with a queen. Not that the queen would visit Longley, but Princess Anne had stopped once, pretending interest in the opening exhibit of hunting paintings before moving on to the next county for the Beresford Hunt.

The Longfords and the Windsors were not exactly on speaking terms. Not since 1902, when the seventh earl—Lizzie's great-grandfather—had made his feelings known about the royal family. In their royal presence. Directly to their royal ears. Since then the royal backs had been turned. The main branch of Longfords, direct descendants of William the Conqueror, had lived happily in shabby splendor at Longley House, while the place crumbled around them.

Elizabeth ran a brush through her shoulder-length hair, then tugged it into a knot at the top of her head.

"M'lady." Peggie addressed her from the doorway. "You're wanted downstairs."

She smoothed her skirt and hurried to the door. "Has Lord Anthony arrived?"

The maid shook her head. "No."

"He should have been here by now."

Peggie shrugged. "No sign of him, but I'll let you know as soon as he steps through the door."

"Don't worry about that. Just make sure you show him to his room as soon as he arrives. His clothes are ready?"

"Yes. Ironed them all myself."

"Good. Now all we have to do is convince our guests that they are having a genuine glimpse into English country life. Tell Pattie to wait a little longer until she serves tea. The sandwiches are made and ready to be sliced, and there's a fruit salad waiting in the refrigerator. I'll be down as soon as I've checked the rooms."

"It's not the food," the plump young woman said, shaking her head and disturbing the red curls piled on top. "An American lady is acting strangely."

"An American lady? I thought the tours ended yesterday." She'd deliberately planned to hold this weekend after the daily influx of tourists had stopped.

"It's the last one. There was some mix-up in the plans," the maid replied. "Miss Dianne promised she'd have them out of here by four, but the American lady swooned."

"The poor thing." Elizabeth looked at her watch. She had ten, no, nine minutes before her guests arrived. "Where is she?"

"In the blue bedroom. Mr. Ruckles told me to fetch you. He said he had no patience for silly maids."

Mr. Ruckles had no patience for tourists, either. Or granddaughters of earls who thought they could run the family home, turn enough of a profit to fix the roof, restore the paintings and keep the place from falling down around their heads.

Elizabeth hurried out of her room and down the long hall of the first—and private—floor. She took the servants stairs to the first floor, which put the blue bedroom three doors down on the right.

"Sammy, I'm fine," a pretty, silver-haired lady insisted from the floor.

"Don't move," said a man with a set of wide shoulders beneath a white knit shirt. He was kneeling beside the woman, and he held her hand. "You're still very pale."

Elizabeth hurried into the room. "Can I help you?"

The man turned, handsome and frowning. Dark eyes examined her, and his expression grew fierce. "My mother fainted."

"The queen," the woman said, staring up at Lizzie with watery blue eyes and colorless skin.

"I'm Lady Elizabeth Longford."

"Of course. My destiny," the woman murmured and closed her eyes.

"Destiny?"

"She listened to a fortune-teller in Canterbury," the man said, as if that explained everything. "Mom?"

"I'll call a doctor."

"An ambulance would be better."

"We're quite a distance from a hospital, Mr. uh—"

"Martin. Sam Martin."

The woman kept her eyes closed and spoke in a soft voice. "Are you married, my dear?"

She looked down at the woman. "You're not with the group of travel agents?"

The blue eyes opened and assessed her. "No wedding ring."

"Mother," Sam interrupted. "This is none of your business."

Elizabeth touched his arm, then wished she hadn't. He was warm and solid and he didn't look as if he appreciated the gesture of compassion. "It's all right."

"Perfect," the old lady murmured, then closed her eyes again.

"Is there something I can do for you to make you more comfortable?" She didn't know why the woman intrigued her, but there was something about her that made Elizabeth want to protect her.

"The bed," Betsy said, her eyes closed. "Perhaps if I could get off this floor. The perfume—"

"Perfume?" Elizabeth sniffed the air. She smelled dust and a trace of mildew, but no perfume. "Mr. Martin, could you carry your mother upstairs to the private rooms? She would be more comfortable there, and then we could call—"

"Of course," he said, lifting his mother easily into his arms.

"No," the old woman said. "The blue bed. I can't—I can't move far."

"All right."

"The bed?" Ruckles's eyes grew wide. "She can't—"

"Of course she can," Elizabeth said firmly.

The man hesitated. "It won't fall apart?"

"No. I don't think so."

"Madame." Ruckles cleared his throat. "May I suggest—"

"Moving those ropes? Of course. What a good idea." Lizzie moved them herself, allowing Sam Martin to place his mother on the bed.

"Perfect," the lady said, smiling a sweet smile toward Lizzie. "You are so kind."

"How are you feeling now?"

Her tiny fingers stroked the satin material that covered the mattress. "Lovely."

"I think we should call a doctor," Sam Martin said again.

"Nonsense," the woman said. "There's nothing wrong with me, Sam."

"You fainted. You're in a stranger's bed."

"Not a stranger's bed, dear." She gave the young woman a conspiratorial smile. "Queen Elizabeth's bed."

"I hate to disappoint you, Mrs. Martin," Elizabeth began, ignoring the way Ruckles cleared his throat once again. "This was never Queen Elizabeth's bed, but it is a lovely sixteenth—"

"Oh, yes, it is." Mrs. Martin looked across the room to the huge portrait. "I think she liked this room very much."

Elizabeth didn't know what to say. Longford House had only been open to tourists for three seasons, but she'd discovered that Americans tended to get awfully excited sometimes. And over the oddest things.

Her son patted her hand. "Mother, I think you'd better rest now."

"Merciful heavens," another elderly woman moaned. "If we're late for the bus, Miss Dianne is going to get mad."

"We will notify her of the delay," Elizabeth promised, nodding toward Ruckles.

Ruckles lifted his chin and cast a chilly look over all of them. "Begging your pardon, m'lady, but I am in the middle of chapter three."

"It can wait a bit longer." The man was going to drive her to drink. Lord knows there was enough brandy stored in the wine cellar to make the job easy.

He sighed, a great big dramatic sigh. "Perhaps if you would care to tell me what time you are to meet Miss Dianne?"

"Four o'clock," the woman said worriedly. "Wasn't that right, Sam?"

"Yes."

The butler, looking very disgusted with the activities around him, nodded. "I will see that she is informed of the, ah, problem."

Mr. Martin hesitated. "How far are we from London?"

"Approximately one hundred miles," Elizabeth replied. He really was handsome, in that very physical American way. The expression in those dark brown eyes held genuine concern for his mother, and the gentle way he stroked her hand tugged at her heart. She hid a sigh, wondered what it would be like to be loved like that, then pushed the thought out of her head. Motherhood would come later. And so would all of the other things that went with it, such as love and marriage with the perfect man.

The woman with the cane sat in a chair by the door and tapped her brochure with nervous fingers. Sam Martin left his mother's side to go over and speak to her in words too soft for Elizabeth to hear. The woman nodded, and Mr. Martin helped her to her feet and guided her out the door, giving her over to the care of Ruckles as he left the room at the same time.

Mr. Martin appeared to be quite accustomed to managing people and giving instructions, she noted, and when he headed toward her she could only hope he wouldn't start telling her what to do also.

"Thanks for your help," he said to her.

"You're quite welcome," was all she could manage in reply. He was very tall, and up close he was even more handsome than she'd first noticed. High cheekbones, dark eyebrows and a beautifully shaped mouth definitely was an appealing combination. He looked solid and earthy, the kind of man who worked outside.

"Marjoram," Mrs. Martin announced, opening her eyes and turning to Elizabeth. "That's what I smell. Are you cooking something?"

"Not right now." She sniffed the air. "I'm afraid I don't notice the odor, Mrs. Martin. And the kitchens are quite a distance away."

The woman frowned. "Well, it's not as strong as it was before, thank goodness."

Ruckles returned. "M'lady, your guests have begun to arrive."

Which meant she needed to greet them. They expected authenticity, and authenticity was exactly what they were going to receive. Damn Anthony. She should have known better than to rely on him, but she'd had very few choices left. And too much depended upon this weekend.

Elizabeth leaned forward and patted Mrs. Martin's soft hand. "Please rest for as long as you need. I'll send up some tea. Ruckles, would you see to it that Mrs. Martin is not disturbed by other visitors?"

The butler's frown deepened. "Tea, m'lady? In *here?*"

She prayed for patience and assumed an authoritative attitude that she certainly didn't feel. "I'm certain that in five hundred years, it won't be the first time that tea has been served in this particular room." She turned to Mrs. Martin. "I'm afraid I have work to do and can't stay, but please, do not leave until you feel quite ready."

"Thank you. You've been so kind."

Elizabeth turned to the son, who happened to be standing terribly close to her side. "If you need anything you have only to tell the maid or Ruckles."

"Is there somewhere I can rent a car?"

"Ruckles will find out for you," she promised, "but we're quite a distance from a city. Perhaps your mother will feel able to join the tour by four."

"Perhaps." He sounded so grim she could tell that prospect didn't appeal to him.

"If you will excuse me," she said, trying to step around him.

"Of course." He moved, and his gaze swept over her clothing. "Do you always dress like that?"

"Yes," Elizabeth fibbed, lifting her chin. "It seems to amuse the tourists."

He surprised her by laughing. "Yes," he said, "I'm sure it does."

She fought the urge to tug her bodice higher over her breasts and instead swept past him out of the room.

2

"NOTHING LIKE THIS has ever happened before," Miss Dianne declared, looking at Sam. "No one has ever crawled into a display bed and refused to get out. Except once—" Her gaze turned speculative, and Sam took a step backward.

"Nothing like this has ever happened to my mother before," he said.

"She's not getting out of that bed, you said?"

"Right. She's having dizzy spells."

"She cannot remain in the bed, Sam. It's not as if Longley House is the Ritz and you've simply taken a room for the night. The bed is *priceless*."

He knew that, but he didn't like the way she said it, as if she was more concerned with the bed than she was with his mother's welfare. "She's staying there for now, until she feels well enough to get up."

Dianne sighed and turned to Betsy. "Mrs. Martin, would you like me to call a physician? We could take you to hospital."

"No, thank you." His mother smiled her artificial

smile at the tour guide, who wasn't fooled for a minute.

"Now, Mrs. Martin, surely you understand that you cannot remain in a sixteenth-century bed in Longley House. It simply won't do."

"Dianne, dear," his mother said softly, "I really don't feel like arguing with you about this. Sam will take care of everything. You don't have to...worry."

"And if you're not better by the time we leave, we must call an ambulance. It's what we do in emergencies like these."

Sam broke in. "I've already considered that, but my mother is feeling a little better." He looked at his watch. "We still have time."

"Yes," Dianne conceded. "I'll check back with you at half past three. Hopefully your mother will be feeling more like herself by then, and if not, we can call a physician to have a look. I can't possibly delay the tour, and Longley House closes at four."

"I wouldn't dream of holding up the tour," Betsy declared in a soft voice. "It just wouldn't do."

Dianne sighed. "Perhaps you can catch up with us in Bath."

"That's a good idea," Betsy said. "Maybe you should all just go on ahead without us."

Sam was thinking the exact same thing. They could go straight to London, see a doctor and then take the next available flight home.

Betsy, unlike her son, was having a good day. Her "destiny" wore white muslin, creamy pearls and the smile of an angel. Lady Elizabeth, with the carriage of a queen and the grace of an aristocrat, had welcomed her to Longley House and promised that a maid would see to her every need.

Betsy was in heaven.

It had all come to her in the blue bedroom. Oh, the dizziness was still there, simmering under the surface whenever she moved her head too fast or closed her eyes, but the cloying scent of spice, or whatever it was, had lessened. The butler had struggled to open a window; the lady of the house had promised tea. The oversexed tour guide had finally left the bedroom, after promising to arrange to have their bags removed from the bus.

"Do you have any pain in your chest?"

Betsy shook her head. "No, Sammy. Not a twinge. It was just the strangest thing—"

"Miss Martin?" The maid held a tray piled high with china and food. "Lady Liz said you needed a cup of tea."

Sam frowned as Betsy sat up, but he piled dusty pillows behind her back. "This bed could use some work."

"It's terribly old, it is," the maid agreed, stepping into the room. "'Twas said that the Virgin Queen herself slept in this room, but 'twas nothing but a story after all.''

"She never visited here?"

She placed the tea tray on a nearby table and poured a cup for Betsy. "No, ma'am. It's said she visited the other Longford house, Bates Hall, many times, but this was the old earl's country home, and he wasn't much for entertaining out here. Milk and sugar, ma'am?"

"Sugar, please. One lump is fine."

"Sir?" The maid poured a cup and waited.

"No, thanks."

"Really, Sam. When are you going to get the chance to drink tea in a place like this again?"

The maid picked up an empty cup and waited for his answer. Sam retrieved the chair by the door and carried it to the side of the bed, then sat down. "Just sugar, then," he said, and thanked the maid for her trouble. "And doing this again isn't something I intend to do."

"Try some cakes, too, sir. And some of Lady Elizabeth's scones."

Betsy eyed the raisin-dotted pastry. "She bakes them herself?"

"Yes, ma'am."

"Lovely."

"Will there be anything else, ma'am?"

"No, thank you. Please tell Lady Elizabeth how grateful we are for her hospitality."

"I will. She's a bit busy right now, you know, with the guests arriving for the weekend and all."

Betsy took a sip of the her tea and watched as Sam did the same. "She entertains a lot?"

"Oh, she's not entertaining, ma'am. It's work." The maid smiled as she stood in the doorway. "She makes the tea and sees to the rest. Everyone likes to meet the lady of the manor." With that, the maid disappeared into the hall, but the sound of her shoes on the marble tile echoed for long minutes.

"I still think we should send for a doctor," Sam said, his expression worried. "Are you sure you're not having chest pains?"

"Not a one. It was just that odd sensation, when I looked at the portrait."

"Please don't tell me you're getting psychic in your old age."

"I've always been a practical woman," she informed her son. "I haven't exactly swooned too many times in my life, you know."

"That's what worries me. As soon as we return to London we should see a doctor."

"We'll be home in a few days. I can wait until we get back home. I'd rather see my own doctor, anyway. I'm too old to have strangers poking and prodding me."

"We'll see. If there are any more of these incidents, then you'll see a doctor. No matter where we are."

"All right," she agreed, hoping to appease him and change the subject to something more agreeable. Like love. "What did you think of Lady Lizzie?"

"Sounds like the name of a collie. 'Lady Lizzie, here girl.'"

"Sam!"

"She seems very...polite. I can't imagine anyone letting a stranger crawl into one of their antique beds, but I guess she didn't want a lawsuit, either."

"It's not like you to be cynical."

"Maybe I'm changing. No more Mr. Nice Guy." He drank most of his tea in several gulps. "I could use a decent cup of coffee, and don't tell me that you don't want one, too."

"I'm getting used to tea. Have a scone."

He took one. "Baked by the princess herself, according to the maid."

"Something else you don't believe?"

"If the lady of the manor gets her hands dirty in the kitchen of this mausoleum, I'll have to see it to believe it." He looked at his watch. "The bus is going to be leaving in an hour. Are you sure you don't want to try to travel? We could be in a nice, clean hotel tonight. And tomorrow afternoon we'll arrive in London."

"I don't feel well enough to climb on a bus right now." Truthfully, the thought of the bus made her feel queasy.

"I'll talk to Dianne and find out if there is anyplace to stay in the village. That strange butler ought to be able to tell me how to rent a car."

"Okay," Betsy said, replacing her teacup and napkin on the tray. "I think I'm going to lie down for a few minutes."

"Will you be all right if I go downstairs to talk to the butler?"

"Don't leave me quite yet, Sammy," she said, eyeing the picture of Queen Elizabeth again. The woman looked as if she could come right out of the canvas and start scaring the living daylights out of everyone in England. "I'd feel better if you stayed, at least for a little while."

"All right," he agreed, as she had known he would.

Betsy shivered and snuggled under the wool throw the maid had brought. "What happened to Grace?"

"Ruckles took her to find some of the others. I promised to tell her how you were doing."

Betsy closed her eyes and wondered how the fortune-teller had known. "You should have had your tarot cards read, too, Sammy."

"You haven't met your destiny, Mother."

She pretended to sleep. She needed time to think.

Her destiny had been shown to her, and now all she had to do was figure out how to hang on to it.

ELIZABETH PAUSED in the black-and-white tiled foyer in front of the grand ballroom. She could hear the low murmur of conversation and the gentle clatter of teacups.

"They've been asking for you, m'lady," Pattie said, coming out of the room with an empty silver tray.

"And here I am. We've had a slight upset."

"I heard. What are you going to do?"

"Skip the blue bedroom on the tour, of course. We'll keep the door shut. Put up a sign that says Under Refurbishment until the Americans are able to leave. Where's Anthony?"

Pattie, older sister to Peggie, rolled her eyes. "No sign of him, m'lady."

"He should have been here an hour ago." She needed a Lord Longford and she needed one right away. "I'll greet the guests, pour tea and then show them to their rooms."

"What about Lord Longford?"

"I'll say he's been delayed. Estate business."

Pattie's eyes clouded with confusion. "Yes, ma'am."

"Don't worry, Pattie. We'll get through this. Didn't we spend last winter planning this? If the travel agents like our 'Life at Longley' weekend idea, things will begin to improve around here.''

The maid didn't look convinced. ''Life at Longley *needs* to improve.'' She sighed.

Lizzie couldn't agree more. She'd spent the last two years trying to prevent Longley from being sold. She'd spent countless hours begging the trustees of her grandfather's estate into giving her a chance to preserve the family home.

Since she was the only remaining heir interested in saving the house, the white-haired men hadn't exactly had a choice. And they were happy to delay what they felt was inevitable: selling Longley, which was the best solution.

So Lizzie lifted her chin, swept into the ballroom and greeted her guests. There were ten travel agency representatives from the United States and Canada, all women of varying ages, shapes and sizes.

Lizzie had memorized their names and occupations, but putting faces to the names would take a little practice. Barbara Canfield, the tall woman with the silver hair, was from New York. Dorla Long, a travel agent from Boston, appeared to be cheerful and content to look around the room. Karen Carmichael and Melissa Lee seemed quiet and self-sufficient; they were history professors from Yale who led summer tours. Phyllis Nolan, a self-possessed blonde, led student tours. Rhonda Cummings, an older lady with a grandmotherly air, owned one of the busiest agencies in New York City. Nancy Mack had a chain of agencies that stretched across the Midwest, Jackie Bertrand represented a company who published tourist guide books, and there were two dark-haired women who had explained they operated an internet travel agency and travel club. Lizzie glanced at her notes. Yes, Ellen Lizotte and Marje Fridrich were from Phoenix.

Lizzie answered their questions about the house, poured more tea and showed them to their rooms in the east wing. Thanks to her great-grandmother's love of comfort, the guest bedrooms were large and beautifully furnished. Dressing rooms had been turned into bathrooms fifty years ago, and with luck the plumbing would hold up for a few more years.

Her guests seemed thrilled with everything so far, so Lizzie left them to unpack while she went to find the missing ingredient for the weekend: a husband.

THE AMERICAN was using the phone in her office, but from the look on his face he didn't appear to be having any luck finding a car. "Tomorrow?" He frowned. "I really need to rent a car this afternoon." He listened, wrote down something on a pad, then thanked whoever he was talking to, before replacing the receiver.

"Trouble?" she asked.

"Yeah. Is there a place around here where my mother and I can spend the night? A bed and breakfast or a hotel?"

Elizabeth thought for a minute. "I have a list somewhere, but it's the middle of September. The season is pretty much over, and things are closing. Or completely booked ahead of time."

"Damn. The tour has left without us, my mother is still asleep upstairs, and I'm stranded in the middle of England without a car."

"Look," she said, feeling sorry for him, "Give me a minute to ring London and then I'll find that list for you."

"Thanks." He moved away from the desk, but he didn't leave the room. Lizzie turned her back on him and dialed Anthony's number. Relief swept over her when the phone was picked up on the third ring.

"Anthony?"

A woman's amused voice replied, "Sorry, luv, but he's not here right now. Can I take message for you?"

There were any number of things she wanted to say, but Elizabeth held her tongue. "Would you remind him to call Longley House, please?"

"Sure, as soon as he comes back, but he's on assignment in Tunisia. As soon as he returns I'll have him ring you up."

"Thank you." She hung up the phone and took

several deep, calming breaths. Anthony had promised. Anthony didn't keep promises. She should have known better, but desperation had clouded her judgment.

"Bad news?"

"Yes." She turned and forced a smile. "My ex-husband forgot he was to be here for the weekend."

"You always invite your ex-husband to visit?"

"We weren't married long enough to create a lot of hard feelings," she explained. "And he was supposed to help me by filling in as a husband."

He raised an eyebrow.

"For the travel agents," she replied. "For the Life at Longley weekend. I thought authentic country estate weekends would appeal to tourists. I've invited representatives from the top firms to come and see what we had to offer."

"Including artificial lords?"

"Oh, he's the real thing. The ladies would have loved him."

"Yeah. They usually do. And that's how you became Lady Longford? I thought you were one of the family."

"I am." Elizabeth struggled to change the subject. "How is your mother feeling?"

"She's still asleep."

Elizabeth rummaged through the stacks of papers until she found a brochure, then she handed it to

Sam. "Here's the list of lodgings. It may be a little dated, but someone might have a room."

"Thanks. I appreciate the help." He moved toward the telephone. "You don't mind if I make the calls in here?"

"No."

"Thanks," he replied, glancing once again at her dress. "What century are you supposed to be in?"

"Oh. You mean my dress?"

He nodded.

"Late seventeen, early eighteen hundreds."

"Jane Austen."

"Yes. She's very popular again."

"I heard."

"You'll have to excuse me. I have to see to my guests." And yet she didn't feel at all like leaving the room. Sam Martin, in his blue jeans and tennis shoes, was oddly sexy. And very attractive.

"Without Lord—what's his name?"

"Anthony, Lord Longford." Maybe it was the brown eyes. There was kindness there and amusement. That expression, combined with the broadest set of shoulders she'd seen since the local rugby team held their annual picnic on the east lawn, was positively mesmerizing.

"Stood up by your ex-husband. I'd say you were having a bad day."

"I've had worse," she said, and hurried out the door.

"HAS HE ARRIVED?" the maid whispered to someone who had entered the room.

A similar voice, with what Betsy guessed held an Irish lilt, replied. "No. It doesn't look like he's going to, either, more's the pity."

Betsy kept her eyes closed and pretended to be asleep. Who were the maids talking about?

"Is Lady Liz very upset?"

"He never had any sense," the other muttered, and Betsy heard the gentle rattle of the tea tray next to the bed and the soft patter of footsteps heading away from the bed. She couldn't help it; she had to know what was going on, so she opened her eyes and let out a little moan, just so the maids would hear.

"Ma'am?" The maid peered anxiously down at her. "Are you feeling a bit better now?" one asked.

"Just a bit," Betsy admitted. It wouldn't do to recover too quickly. She eased herself into a sitting position while one of the maids positioned a dusty blue pillow behind her back. "Are you Peggy or Pattie?"

"Pattie, ma'am. Is that better?"

"Thank you so much." Betsy eased back against the pillow and relaxed. So this is what it would be like to have servants. She had always wondered. Her gaze went across the room to the forbidding portrait of Elizabeth I. Now there was a woman who knew how to control her own destiny. A woman of the nineties could take lessons.

"You're quite welcome."

"Tell me, Pattie, who were you talking to just now?"

"My sister. She just finished checking on the others."

"Who is the man who hasn't arrived? He sounds mysterious."

"Not so mysterious." Pattie sank into the chair by the bed. "Aw, it feels good to sit down for a bit. I've been on my poor little feet all day."

"This is a very large house."

"Not as large as some," the maid declared. "Longley tries to compete with places like Chatsworth and Leeds Castle, but it's terribly hard. We're not big enough."

"So, who is Lady Liz expecting?"

"Lord Anthony." The maid sighed. "They were married once upon a time, but it didn't last long. He was supposed to help her this weekend, play the lord of the manor for her guests."

Betsy thought about that for a few seconds before asking her next question. "Why?"

"It's the idea, you see. Lord and lady of Longley

House, a weekend of country living, all that. It's an experiment, Lady Liz says. If it works, we can make enough money to keep the house open. We need to find something special, something that makes us different, Lady Liz says. And Lord Anthony agreed to help.''

"And if this weekend idea doesn't work?"

The maid sighed. "Lady Liz doesn't like to talk about that. There's people who would buy this place for a hotel.''

"But this is her home." Betsy's gaze went to the portrait again. The queen seemed to be staring right into her eyes, as if daring her to solve the problem.

Pattie stood. "Guess I'd better be going along. We've the guests settled into their rooms and they've had their tea. We've tours to give and dinner to prepare.''

"And I'm causing you more work. I'm sorry."

She smiled. "You can't help swooning, Mrs. Martin. Just take care of yourself. It's a shame your bus left without you.''

No, it wasn't. It was destiny. Fate. And possible low blood pressure. "Have you seen my son?"

"He was downstairs a while ago. Ringing up hotels, I think.'' She winked at Betsy. "He's a fine-looking man, your son is.''

It was amazing how some ideas materialized.

Right out of the blue, fully formed and perfect. "He's rather...lordlike, don't you think?"

Pattie hesitated. "You mean—?"

Ruckles appeared at the door. "Pattie! You're wanted in the kitchen."

The maid turned, nodded and quickly stepped away from the bed. "Lady Liz needs a miracle, Mrs. Martin."

"Lady Elizabeth needs more than a miracle, Pattie. She needs a *man*."

"ABSOLUTELY NOT." Sam stood his ground. He wasn't rescuing any more women—the senior citizens brigade he'd been shepherding was enough. He was not going to let himself be taken advantage of again. No matter how beautiful the woman who wept into tissues, no matter if lovely eyelashes grew damp with tears and soft hands held his and sweet lips spoke the words "Please, Sam."

And then there was his mother. He wasn't going to cave in, no matter how much guilt she laid on him, either. He was tired of being nice.

"Please, Sam," his mother said in a stern voice. It was more like a demand, spoken without tears and hand holding.

"No."

"It's for a good cause."

"It's the fainting spell, isn't it?" He paced across

the room at the foot of the hideous blue bed, paused before the portrait, then turned to his mother. "You've lost brain cells. You're not yourself."

"I'm in perfect—well, almost perfect condition," Betsy declared. "There's nothing wrong with my mind." She winced as she sat on the edge of the bed. "I'm just feeling a little...weak."

He didn't like the sound of that. "How weak?"

"Just a little shaky. Just the thought of walking down the stairs—"

"I'll carry you."

"And getting into a car—"

"The gardener is going to drive us to a hotel about fifteen miles south of here. It just so happens he lives nearby, and we're lucky to get a ride with him."

Betsy frowned. "I like this bed."

"You can't stay in that dirty bed."

"It's not dirty. It's old. And I think the queen slept in it."

"The queen?" came a voice behind him. "Which one?"

Sam turned around as a group of women entered the room. One of them, an imposing silver-haired woman with a clipboard, eyed Betsy curiously. "Which queen slept in this bed?" she asked once again, her pen poised above the paper.

"Queen Elizabeth I, of course," Betsy replied without blinking an eye.

"Mother," Sam cautioned, but his warning was ignored.

"How wonderful," the woman said, and turned to the portrait. Three other women stood near it, talking in low tones and sending admiring glances toward the furniture and tapestry. "I had no idea."

"Not many people do."

"Have we disturbed you? We had no idea this was a private bedroom," a younger woman said to Betsy. "I'm so sorry."

"It's not," Sam said. "My mother felt ill and we had to—"

"We had to make other arrangements," Betsy broke in. "I do love this room, though. Don't you?"

The women nodded, and the one with the clipboard scribbled something. "How wonderful," she said again, "that the house is used by the family. You *are* the family, I assume?"

"No," Sam tried. "We're—"

"Stop it, dear," Betsy interrupted once again. "You are our guests, the travel people, aren't you?" They nodded. Betsy smiled a particularly regal smile that oozed charm. "We are so pleased to have you visit us this weekend. Lady Elizabeth has planned such lovely entertainments."

"And you are?" clipboard woman asked.

"Another Elizabeth," his mother murmured modestly. "And this is my son, Lord Longford."

"What?" Sam was certain he hadn't heard her correctly.

The women's eyes widened. One of them curtsied.

"I'm not—" he tried to say, but his mother took his hand.

"Sam, dear, I'm feeling ill again. Could you ask Pattie to send up tea?"

"You don't sound British," the woman with the pen said. "Were you educated in the States?"

"We lived there for many years," Betsy confided. "Family problems. You know how that is. It's *very* complicated."

The four women nodded. Everyone knew how complicated families could be. "We should leave you alone," one of them said. "We hope you feel better."

"Thank you, my dear," Betsy said. "Enjoy yourselves here at Longley."

"I'm sure we will," another said.

Before Sam could shoo the women out of the room and convince his mother to leave this crazy house, Lizzie swept into the room, clearly unaware the effect her half-bared bosom would have on a man. The pearl necklace nestled against her throat, and she'd added little earrings that fluttered as she walked toward her guests. "Ms. Canfield? Ms. Long? We've been searching for you. I was afraid you'd been lost."

"Oh, no, Lady Elizabeth. We met your mother-in-law and were visiting."

"My mother-in-law?"

Betsy waved. "Darling, I'm afraid I'm still in this bed. Your company caught me at an awkward moment."

Sam tried to find his voice. Cool blondes had always appealed to him, and this lady was no exception. "I'll explain," Sam offered. "And we'll be leaving as soon as possible."

"Leaving?" Ms. Long asked. "Why?"

His mother had the answer. "Leaving the room, dear. Not Longley House!"

Lizzie smiled at the four women who looked thrilled to have met the Lord Longford and his mother. "Tea is being served in the library. If you'd like to join the others, Ruckles will show you the way."

"This is just like that 'Pride and Prejudice' mini-series." The dark-haired woman sighed. "I can't wait to tell everyone about meeting a lord."

"I preferred *Emma*." The clipboard woman needed to make her opinion known.

The others nodded and obediently left the room.

"Lovely." Betsy sighed, once the three of them were alone. Lizzie closed the door and approached the bed.

"What on earth is going on?"

"My mother is clearly out of her mind."

Betsy patted Elizabeth's hand. "Your guests are lovely."

"They shouldn't have been in here."

"And they shouldn't have been told lies, either," Sam scolded his mother. "What am I going to do with you?"

"Now, dear, don't fret." She turned to the young woman. "You'd be happy to have a Lord Longford for the weekend," his mother announced. "Wouldn't you?"

"Excuse me?"

"The maid explained everything, so of course I thought it made sense to have my son—you have to admit he's a commanding kind of guy—to play the part of the lord. It would solve all of our problems."

"*Our* problems?" Sam asked, shoving his hands in the pockets of his jeans. "I don't have any problems."

Elizabeth glared at him. "You're stuck in the middle of England with an ailing mother who faints at the sight of Queen Elizabeth and tells strangers that she's the mother of a lord. I'd say that's a problem."

The lady, unfortunately, had a point. "I'll get her out of here," he promised. "Right away. The gardener is going to drive us to a hotel in South Middletown. We both want to thank you for your patience and your help."

"Oh, Sam," Betsy muttered, "you don't have to sound so formal. Lady Elizabeth needs help this weekend. You're the answer to her prayers."

She took a step backward. "Mrs. Martin, I couldn't possibly—"

"Of course you could," his mother insisted. "Sam would make a great lord."

Elizabeth shot Sam a look that said *help me*.

"No," said Sam. "I would not. We're going to leave here immediately, before our hostess is embarrassed any more."

The lady turned and slowly assessed him, from the top of his head to his running shoes. She shook her head. "He's too American looking. And, of course, the accent—"

"You could say Lord Longford was educated in Boston," his mother suggested. "A *very* well-traveled man, in the true Longford tradition."

Sam frowned at both of them. "What does 'too American looking' mean?"

Elizabeth was clearly trying to be tactful. "I think it's a matter of attitude. Could you be a bit more reserved? Bored, even?"

He looked down into those blue eyes. "No."

Betsy clapped her hands in delight. "See? He can be haughty when he wants to."

"I wasn't—"

"Maybe," Lady Liz said, staring at his chest and

then his waist. "I don't know if the clothes would fit."

"I'm not wearing a costume and I'm not playing a lord."

The little blonde turned to Betsy. "You got me into this, Mrs. Martin. What do you want?"

"The blue bed for the weekend. Maid service. A ride to the nearest train station Sunday afternoon, and I play the part of your mother-in-law. If," she said, her gaze darting to Sam, "if I feel well enough, that is."

"I'm afraid I don't have any choice." Lady Liz turned back to Sam. "I'll show you your room. Dinner is at seven. We'll need an hour or two to educate you on Longley, but don't worry. I'll answer most of the questions. You simply have to sit at the head of the table and be polite."

"I don't want to do this," he said, feeling as if no one was listening to anything he said.

"Sure you do, Sam," his mother declared. "It'll be fun."

"Your mother has gotten us into this. I won't look like a liar or a fool in front of the people who can make or break my business." Lizzie stuck out her hand for him to shake. "Do we have a deal, Mr. Martin?"

"Call me Sam." Her skin was soft. As he had known it would be.

"I should call you 'my lord.'"

"That's a new one."

She smiled and withdrew her hand. "You'll have to grow accustomed to it, don't you see?"

"I see." And he did.

The English were all insane.

And he'd just become one of them.

3

"I NEED A DRINK," declared the new lord.

"Follow me." Figuring they both had the right to indulge, Lizzie led him downstairs to the library. She rang a bell on the wall, and Ruckles appeared almost instantly, making Liz wonder if the old man had been in the library researching his book when he should have been seeing to the guests. There had been no Closed sign in front of the door to the blue bedroom. Guests were roaming around the public part of the house, and they might have questions.

The butler bowed, his long face solemn.

"What would you like?" she asked the American.

"Scotch, if you have it. A little water, no ice."

"Fine. And I'll have a glass of wine. The Beaujolais, please."

The butler nodded and left the room.

"Is he an actor or a real butler?"

"He's authentic. Generations of butlers named Ruckles have served the family. He, however, doesn't want to be a butler." Lizzie sank into a maroon leather chair and gestured for her guest to sit in the one across from her.

"He should be playing the part of the lord."

She smiled wryly. "I thought of that, but the guests had already seen him as the butler. He can give you lessons on attitude."

"No kidding." He leveled his dark-eyed gaze on her. "This isn't going to work, you know. I'm a carpenter, I build things." He held out his hands, palms up, to her. "Feel me."

She wished he'd used a different phrase. She'd been married for six months, three years ago, and she'd never had a man look at her and demand to be felt.

Which could have been the problem with her marriage.

Lizzie touched his palms with tentative fingers. The skin was callused and rough, his wrists brown from working outside. "And your point is?"

Ruckles cleared his throat, making Lizzie jump. She dropped her hands and leaned back while the butler put the tray of drinks on the table between them.

"Thanks," Sam said. "Do you have a first name?"

Ruckles glared at him. "No."

"Mrs. Martin has told our guests that she is my mother-in-law and Mr. Martin is Lord Longford. Mr.

Martin is going to act as my, er, Longley's host for the weekend,'' Lizzie said, taking a sip of her drink.

"You must be joking, m'lady."

"Not at all." Lizzie gave him her most commanding look. "Mrs. Martin will be staying in the blue bedroom and Mr. Martin—" She stopped, since she hadn't given any thought to where she was going to put Sam. The bedrooms, at least the ones prepared for visitors, were occupied.

"Yes, m'lady."

"I'm thinking."

Sam picked up his glass. "Let me leave now, while I can. I can carry my mother over my shoulder and toss her into a car. You do have a car, don't you?"

"Yes, but—"

He leaned forward. "No one is going to believe that I'm Lord Longford."

"No," the butler said. "Of course they're not. Our guests are highly intelligent business people."

Lizzie's heart sank. "Oh, dear. I thought that was the perfect solution."

The American sipped his scotch and seemed satisfied with its taste. "You were under my mother's spell. It happens. Once you regain your senses, you'll see that this will never work."

"If I disappoint my guests, they won't recommend this particular tour to their clients."

"Don't you know any other lords or dukes?"

"Not under seventy years old."

Sam shrugged and took another sip of scotch. "Seems like a lord is a lord. Invite your neighbors over for drinks and let your travel agents mingle with them for an hour."

"That's not what I promised. I need a host, someone whose presence will provide that extra bit of authenticity." She needed someone to help while she was in the kitchen preparing the meals. Damn Anthony. He had agreed to help her. He owed her one bloody weekend. She looked at Sam. "That's you."

Ruckles cleared his throat. "If I may say something, m'lady."

"Sit down," Sam told him. "Have a drink."

"Thank you, sir, but I prefer to stand." He raised his eyebrows at Lizzie as if to say *what else did you expect?*

"Suit yourself, but I think we could use a third opinion here."

"The blue jeans and tennis shoes will have to be removed."

"What?"

The butler almost smiled. "A third opinion, sir."

"I see." Sam looked down at his clothes, then to Lizzie. "Not formal enough for you?"

"I think you look fine," she assured him. "But it

would help if you wore something a little more...lordly."

"You can't pass me off as royalty," he said. "I thought we already determined that. I'm really not any use to you, so as soon as I finish my scotch—which is excellent, by the way—my mother and I will leave."

Ruckles nodded. "You're drinking a very fine unblended, single malt whiskey from the Highlands. And may I contribute an idea, sir?"

"Sure." Sam took another sip of his drink. "I've never tasted anything like this."

Lizzie realized she'd forgotten to drink her wine. And the men had forgotten to include her in the discussion. She leaned back in her chair and waited for her butler to continue. The long-faced man looked almost happy.

"Your being royalty is out of the question," he stated. "And as an aristocrat, a lord, well, your American attributes would certainly hinder a performance of that magnitude. Simply put, you would not be believed. With that said, in all due respect of course, Longley House is in dire need of a host for the weekend. And since Lord Anthony has been indisposed, and Mrs. Martin is ensconced in the blue bedroom, it appears you are of considerable use to Lady Elizabeth after all." He paused dramatically.

"I will educate you as a lord. You will behave as befits Lady Longford's husband."

Lizzie felt a little weak. She could too easily picture the handsome American as a husband, at least in the physical sense. "Ruckles!"

The butler nodded. "I do not condone Lady Elizabeth resorting to deception, something which is beneath her and certainly unflattering. Posing as a husband would naturally allow you the respect due to such a position, but would require deceit and a certain amount of—"

"Stop right there," Sam ordered. He turned to Lizzie. "What the hell is he talking about?"

"There must be other options. I could invite Lord Barth to dinner. He's a bit forgetful, but very charming."

Ruckles cleared his throat. "Your guests have already met Lord Longford."

Sam stared at him. "I don't think any of this is necessary."

Lizzie disagreed. "I need help. You're quite trapped here. It's perfect."

"Excellent," Ruckles said, moving toward the door. "I'll take Mr. Martin's luggage upstairs."

Lizzie tried not to question her own judgment. Maybe this was merely making the most of a difficult situation. "Will you do it, Mr. Martin?"

He sighed. "Call me Sam. And I don't exactly have a choice, do I?"

"You always have a choice."

"Not when you have Betsy Martin for a mother."

BETSY MARTIN was, at that moment, standing at the window overlooking the back gardens. Flowers still bloomed in thick bunches along the gravel walks, and in the distance green fields stretched to a line of thick woods. Paradise, Betsy figured, was an English landscape. She glanced once again at the painting of the queen. The old girl stared back, but Betsy wasn't the least bit intimidated. There was a faint trace of marjoram in the air, but Betsy decided the odor came from the painting, or rather from the magic of the painting, not from some strange ancient combination of paints used in the Elizabethan period of history.

"Well, old girl," Betsy murmured. "If you're haunting this room, this is a good time to prove it."

The painting stayed on the wall, no ghostly currents chilled Betsy's skin. Silence filled the room. The queen wasn't going to talk.

"That's all right," Betsy said. "I can talk enough for both of us." She roamed around the blue and gold room and wondered what it would be like to live in such magnificence. Now she was about to find out. Her son would help the lovely Lady Elizabeth, and the sweet girl was certain to fall in love with him. Everyone loved Sam. He was well mannered and kind, handsome and good-natured. Up until now he'd selected the wrong kind of women to date. Up until now he hadn't met the right one. Up until now he hadn't met his match, his destiny.

Betsy knew that this time Sam had encountered the perfect woman. All he needed was a little help from his mother. Mary always said things fell into place when they needed to; Betsy personally believed that "things" needed a little push.

"Madam?"

Betsy froze.

The old butler cleared his throat. "I trust madam has recovered?"

She turned slowly and tried to look ill by frowning and hunching her shoulders. "I was trying to find the bathroom."

He opened a gold-trimmed door cut into the wall. "I believe you will find everything you need in here."

"Thank you."

"This was once the master suite, before Lady Elizabeth's grandmother passed away. She also preferred to sleep in this room and turned the garderobe into a lavatory."

Betsy shuffled past him and made a show out of turning on the porcelain-handled faucet and splashing her face with cold water. The small room was noth-

ing fancy; in fact, it looked like the bathroom in the
hotel last night. A faded blue towel hung from a glass
bar by the sink, so Betsy dabbed her face with it.
"What was a *garderobe?*"

"Where the knights slept while not guarding their
queen, ma'am."

She could have swooned with joy. A garderobe.
Knights! Her own private bathroom, which she certainly could use after drinking all that tea. Slowly
she walked back to the bed and climbed inside while
Ruckles disappeared into the hall. He reappeared
with her luggage, two bright blue duffle bags, which
he set gingerly inside the door.

"I will send one of the maids to unpack your
things," he said.

She was definitely in the right place. A maid to
unpack! Not even the obviously disproving butler
could quell her joy.

"Thank you."

He nodded, and his gaze shifted to the portrait of
the queen. "It's been said this room is haunted."

"By her?"

"We don't know, madam. Her Majesty never visited Longley."

"She could have."

"It is not documented, madam."

Betsy didn't understand. "Documented? How?"

"Letters, journals, entries in the household accounts. A visit from the queen would have meant tremendous expense. It would not go unrecorded."

"And you would know."

He nodded modestly. "I have been researching the history of the house. For my book."

"You're writing a book?"

Ruckles couldn't hide his pride. "Yes. When I have the time, of course." He sighed. "There is so much to do around here."

"Oh, I'm sure there is. It's such an enormous house." She returned to the bed and perched on the edge of the hard mattress. "Could I read it?"

"I'm only in chapter three, madam. There are boxes of information I haven't been able to catalogue yet."

Betsy would bet her last pair of elastic-waist slacks that Queen Elizabeth had been in this room, in this bed, on this grand estate. "I could help," she offered. "After all, I *am* bedridden for the weekend. I could read through a box or two."

Ruckles's eyebrows lifted. "You are a historian, Mrs. Martin?"

She attempted to look intellectual. "I dabble," she replied, hoping he'd believe such a lie.

He hesitated, but not for long. "I could bring one of the boxes to you. There is a lot of correspondence. Perhaps a magnifying glass would be of assistance."

"Sure. Whatever works."

Ruckles wasn't fooled. "And your son is going to be helping Lady Elizabeth, so I suppose I will not be needed?"

"I think we should leave the young people alone. I'm sure they can muddle along without us."

"Yes, madam. I'm certain you are correct."

Betsy smiled. Butlers were so smart.

"I AM NOT going to wear those things."

"Of course you are," Lady Elizabeth insisted in that soft voice of hers. "That's the costume."

It was time to assert himself, Sam figured. "I don't wear costumes."

"You do after your mother tells my guests that you're Lord Longford."

He sighed and picked up the tan breeches that were draped over a lace-covered bed. "I'm going to look ridiculous."

"Pretend it's Halloween."

He held the pants up to him. "They're going to be too tight."

Lady Liz didn't seem to be concerned. She handed him a brown jacket. "Why don't you try that on and see if it fits? There's a white waistcoat to go underneath, and Ruckles found a white shirt he thinks will fit you."

"And those?" He gestured toward an assortment

of shoes and boots lined up in front of a gleaming chest of drawers.

"You have your pick," she said, bending over to select a shiny pair of black boots. Sam's attention focused on the amazing display of her soft breasts tucked inside the flimsy white material.

"Is that a nightgown or a dress?" he managed to ask.

"A dress," she said as she straightened and handed him the boots.

"You shouldn't bend over in it."

She flushed and tugged at the bodice of her dress to raise the material about one-eighth of an inch higher. "I'm sorry. I'm not used to wearing these clothes, either. I thought it would be a good idea to add some authenticity to the weekend."

They were authentic, all right, from what he'd glimpsed. And so was the reaction he'd had to the sight. Sam gulped and took the boots. "Just don't bend over or your guests will get more than they bargained for."

"Excuse me," the lady said. "I was just trying to help."

"It would help if you didn't fall out of your dress."

She lifted that chin in the air and turned toward the door. "Please be in the drawing room in forty-five minutes. You're to entertain the guests before dinner."

"They're going to ask me questions about the estate."

"*Try* to be charming. Smile and change the subject," she suggested, hurrying to the door. "I'm late." The door slammed behind her, and Sam was left in the empty room to ponder his new wardrobe. He was going to look like Napoleon or King George or one of those portraits that hung above the staircase.

He was going to look like an ass.

And he should be accustomed to it, having been raised by his mother and Aunt Mary, two women with odd notions of how life should be lived. *Gusto* was their middle name, they were fond of telling strangers and friends. *Gusto?* More like *insanity*.

Sam went over to the door and turned the key in the lock. He didn't want any guests walking in on him while he removed his clothes, his *normal* American tourist clothes. He struggled to get into his new pants, despite the odd straps attached to the bottom of the legs. The white shirt was a bit small, but fit well enough, the suspenders were easily adjusted, a white waistcoat buttoned over the shirt. The dark wool jacket was the same as the shirt, a little tight but not impossible. One of the previous earls of Longford must have been the same height, but weighed about twenty fewer pounds. Sam picked up a long length of white fabric, couldn't figure out what to do with it and tossed it back on the bed. He sat down in a little velvet-covered chair and tried on boots until he found a pair that didn't pinch his toes.

Sam stood and surveyed himself in the mirror. He should have known that a quiet little tour of the English countryside would have turned complicated, but in his wildest dreams he wouldn't have thought he'd have ended up wearing tight pants and calling himself "Lord." A discreet knock on the door interrupted his grumbling. "Yes?"

Ruckles answered. "Sir, I've come to assist you with your wardrobe."

Sam unlatched the door and opened it. "I think I'm all set, thanks."

The butler frowned. "Your neck cloth, sir?" He glanced over to the bed. "Ah, there it is. If you will allow me—"

Sam stepped out of the way before the butler ran him down. He shut the door and turned to watch as Ruckles lifted the fabric with careful fingers.

"Of course," the old man grumbled, "I haven't done this in a while. My great-uncle served as valet to the earl of Longford for a brief time. He taught me several of the less-complicated knots."

Sam had no idea what the man was talking about, and said so.

"Please, Mr. Martin, if you would hold still just for a moment or two, I'm certain my memory will return. I will tie it quite neatly around your neck, making certain the folds are correctly aligned."

"You don't have to align anything. I'm not wearing a cravat."

"Of course you are," the butler declared, fumbling with the cloth until it fell to the floor. "As soon as I starch the bloody thing again."

"Skip it." Sam didn't want the prospect of tying a tie to upset the old man any further. "Lady Liz won't notice."

"Possibly not," the older man admitted, standing back to study Sam's attire. "I think she might be pleased to see that your coat fits so nicely. And sir? Your boots should be *inside* your trousers."

Sam looked down. "Inside?"

"Yes, sir. There are straps to go underneath the boots, also."

"This isn't going to work, is it?"

"I must disagree," the butler said, motioning for Sam to sit down in the chair. "You are in need of a bit of information, of course. Allow me to tell you some of the rules a gentleman is expected to obey."

Sam leaned back and prepared to be educated. If he was going to be a lord, he damn well wasn't going to make a fool of himself.

"SHALL I RING THE GONG, m'lady?"

Elizabeth lifted the last pan of roasted chicken from the oven and set it on the counter beside the others. "Not yet, Pattie. Give me five minutes to return to the drawing room."

Peggie hurried into the kitchen, one of the few modern rooms in the house. Elizabeth's grandmother had renovated it forty years ago, and nothing had been changed since. Fortunately the previous lady of the house had believed that her servants needed an efficient room in which to work. She'd installed a huge gas stove, two aluminum sinks and enough countertops to hold food for the queen's army. In the middle of the room was a huge wooden-topped worktable. "M'lady, the table is fixed quite nicely, but I can't find another one of those gold goblets."

Elizabeth shut the oven door and tossed the pot holders on the counter. "There should be twelve. I counted."

Peggie frowned. "Twelve? I thought we were thirteen to dinner, m'lady."

"No." She arranged the platters and removed her apron. "Twelve for dinner tonight. Ten guests and um, Lord Longford and myself." If he was going to be lord of the manor, she may as well begin calling him that.

"Mr. Sam is a handsome one, all right," Peggie giggled.

Her sister agreed. "Oh, my, he certainly is. Aren't we lucky he agreed to stay for the weekend to help us. What are we to call him?"

Elizabeth rearranged the serving dishes in the order of their delivery to the table. "In front of the company, you are to call him 'm'lord.' Otherwise I'm sure 'Mr. Martin' will be appropriate."

"And Mrs. Martin? She won't be joining you at dinner?"

"She will be dining in her room tonight, I'm sure. Don't forget to bring her a tray." The potatoes were tucked in the warming oven with the bread; the wine had been selected by Ruckles; and Mrs. DeVries's elegant desserts tucked carefully on the shelf in the pantry.

Pattie nodded. "I took Mrs. Martin some books from the library, too. She's such a nice lady. Such a shame she's a bit balmy in the head, isn't it?"

"Mrs. Martin simply took ill." She glanced at the clock mounted below the broad beams that held a handful of copper pots. Most of Longley's copper had been donated to the war effort in 1940. Five o'clock. Time to ring the gong and serve drinks to her guests. "Where is the list?"

"Right here, m'lady," one of the young women answered, waving a white sheet of paper.

"Then you know where everything goes."

"Yes."

"And you'll stir the sauce?"

"Yes."

Elizabeth hated to leave the kitchen, but the two sisters smiled and waved her away. She smoothed her skirt as she left the warm kitchen and made her way to the dining room, a route she could negotiate in her sleep: along the stone corridor, avoiding the dampness on the left side; climb the ten stone steps; through the security door; and down a dark passageway to the heavy door at the end. She knew this would work. All the time she'd been basting the chicken and reheating the soup and defrosting the vegetable casseroles, she'd told herself it would work. Surely ten guests could be entertained at an English house party. What could go wrong in three and one-half days?

Sam Martin could, that was certain. He was too handsome. Too American. Too…appealing.

Elizabeth opened the heavy door to the dining room and sighed with satisfaction. The table sparkled with the family's best silver, crystal and china. The fresh flowers arranged in the center lent soft color and elegance, and the ancient table gleamed with fresh polish. She took a deep breath and surveyed one of her favorite rooms as a guest would.

Perfect. The atmosphere was precisely the way she pictured it would be. The gong sounded as Elizabeth straightened her shoulders and headed for the drawing room. Her guests would naturally expect to be greeted before dinner.

Surely she could keep her mind on business and off her handsome new "guest." She'd seen handsome men before. But then she'd admired them from a distance and gone about her business. She'd certainly never pretended to be married to any of them.

Until Sam strolled down the stairs as she crossed the hall. "Lady Elizabeth," he said, coming up to stand before her. "Where do you want me?"

She gulped. What sort of question was that to ask a woman? "The drawing room, please. Ruckles will pour the wine, but you might need to help him mix cocktails should anyone want one."

His dark eyebrows rose. "Lords fix their own drinks?"

"This weekend they do."

"You haven't said anything about my Halloween outfit. Are you pleased, or are you having second thoughts?"

Elizabeth had been trying not to stare lower than those dark brown eyes. "You look…fine."

"Fine?" He shrugged. "Well, I guess that's good enough. This jacket is too small."

"I think it's supposed to fit like that," she said.

He tugged at the neck of his high-buttoned shirt. "I wouldn't be caught dead wearing one of those neck cloths."

"The guests won't notice," she assured him. The ladies would be thrilled with him just the way he was.

And, unfortunately, so was she.

4

"IS YOUR MOTHER joining us for dinner, I hope?"
Barbara Canfield asked, lifting her glass for Ruckles
to refill with white wine.

"Not this evening." Sam poured a generous
amount of scotch into his own crystal glass, then
added water. The old butler had cautioned him
against drinking this stuff straight. "She's been feeling a little under the weather lately."

"I'm sorry. Nothing serious, I hope?"

Sam appreciated her concern. She was the same
silver-haired American who'd carried the clipboard.
"My mother will be up and around by Monday, I'm
sure. She took ill this afternoon, but is perfectly content to rest for a few days." *Perfectly content* was
an understatement, of course. Betsy Martin was in
her glory.

"She seems like a lovely woman. I hope she feels
better soon."

"Thank you. I'll tell her you asked for her." It
was time to change the subject. "Did you enjoy your
tour of the house this afternoon?"

"Oh, yes. It was very interesting."

"You were taking notes. Are you interested in history?"

She shook her head. "No. I send a newsletter of my travels to my clients. It gives them ideas for their own trips, as well as entertaining them with mine."

"I hope you'll enjoy your weekend here."

"It should be quite an experience," she said, as several other women gathered around him to tell him how much they liked his home. *His home.*

Sam nodded as if he'd personally designed every single room in the place himself.

"Elizabeth has worked very hard to restore her family's home," he said. "Having you here means a great deal to her." The four women smiled at him, so he figured he was doing a pretty good job entertaining them. "Where are you from?"

They told him while he replenished their drinks and prayed they wouldn't ask him any questions. He asked them questions instead, about their companies and their jobs, and tried to remember their names. Two were from New York, Dorla lived in Boston, Nancy owned six travel agencies in Chicago. Two young women sat together on a small sofa and talked to each other.

Elizabeth stood nearby. He tried to listen to her conversations with some of the other women—some-

thing about dresses and gardens—and was distracted
by Ruckles's appearance at his shoulder.

"M'lord?"

The four women looked up at him with expectant
expressions, until Sam realized that the butler was
talking to him. He turned. "Yes?"

"You are wanted in the, uh, library."

Which would be fine if he knew where the hell
the library was. "Excuse me," he said to the women,
wondering absently if he should bow. He decided
that would be overkill and settled for a polite nod
and a few steps backward. Luckily Ruckles waited
for him in the hall.

"I don't know where—"

"Sir," the butler said, his voice low. "There is,
of course, no one who wants to see you in the library.
I realized I may have forgotten to tell you where you
would be seated in the dining room. When the gong
rings—"

"I take Lady Elizabeth's arm and lead the way
into dinner." He put his hands on his hips. "Naturally I figure I'll sit at the head of the table."

Ruckles nodded. "I will pour the wine after you
approve it. Lady Elizabeth will signal me as to when
she wants the courses served."

"Yeah. I'm sure she will." The beautiful Lady Liz
no doubt was used to giving orders and having them
obeyed. He looked around the marble foyer toward

the main staircase. "How do I reach my mother's room from here? I should check on her before dinner. She didn't answer my knock a little while ago."

"Perhaps she was napping," the butler suggested. "Your mother was served a dinner tray in, ah, her room and requested she not be disturbed until morning."

Which was smart of her. He could easily change his mind after one dinner as lord of the manor and pack their bags. Still, he didn't like the idea of his mother up there in that room alone. "I think I'll look in on her, anyway."

"I spoke to Mrs. Martin an hour ago, and I will send Pattie to look in on her. You will, of course, be notified should your mother request your assistance."

Since Betsy had already requested his assistance enough for one day, Sam decided to agree. "Fine. I'll wait until after dinner."

"You have seven minutes before dinner is served, sir. I suggest we return to the drawing room now." Ruckles hesitated before opening the door. "I also suggest you stand next to Lady Elizabeth and show her those little courtesies a husband shows a wife."

"I see." In other words, he was to act married. The thought was almost enough to make him lose his appetite. Couldn't a man be allowed to be single? He'd been raised by two women—his mother and

Aunt Mary. Two women who had been matchmaking since he was sixteen. He ran his late father's business, he invested his mother's money, but he'd be damned if he'd marry to please his mother. He took a deep breath and entered the room. And then the little blonde looked at him and smiled. There was a worried expression in those blue eyes he wished he could erase, so he returned the smile and walked toward her.

He let his gaze sweep over her, from the earrings nestled against that silky blond hair to the tips of her gold shoes. A man could certainly be expected to look at his wife that way. He hoped her guests were impressed. "Have I told you how beautiful you look this evening?"

"No."

"Then I apologize, Elizabeth."

She managed a gracious half smile. "Have you met everyone, Sam?"

He smiled at the ladies and hoped he looked aristocratic. "I don't think so."

Elizabeth introduced two women from Connecticut. "Karen Carmichael and Melissa Lee. Professors of history from Yale."

"We're on sabbatical," one of them offered. "Your outfit is very handsome, even without the neck cloth."

"There was no way—"

The sound of a gong interrupted Sam's protest, and the woman patted him on the arm. "Oh, I know. They are so difficult to tie. If you like, I could show you after dinner. Costumes are one of my specialties."

"Thank you, but—"

"Sam?" Elizabeth touched his arm. "Would you like to take Ms. Lee in to dinner?"

"Of course." This wasn't according to the butler's instructions, but Sam tucked the tiny lady's arm through his. "Allow me," he said, leading her through the double set of doors that Ruckles opened to reveal the dining room.

"Oh, my, how lovely," the woman on his arm said with a sigh.

Sam remembered to close his mouth as they approached the table. The room was enormous, dominated by the table in the center. And not just any table, either. Covered with all sorts of fancy plates and glasses, it was the widest piece of furniture Sam had ever expected to pull a chair up to. The floor was gray stone, the fireplace marble and the painting over the mantel some giant portrait of what appeared to be a Longford ancestor. An *unhappy* Longford ancestor. A tapestry hung over the sideboard, on the wall opposite the one with the long windows.

"This is the family dining room," he heard Elizabeth tell Barbara Canfield behind him as he led the awed Ms. Lee to her seat. Each place was identified by a gold-edged card with the guest's name in flowing script. Each place setting held enough silver with which to eat ten meals.

"Oh, my, isn't this lovely," Ms. Lee murmured to no one in particular.

"I'm glad you like it. We don't use the large dining room anymore," his hostess continued softly. "My grandmother eventually used it for storage or for large parties. This is much cozier for dinner. We'll be having most of our meals here."

Sam stood at the head of the table and watched as Elizabeth made sure her guests were settled in their places. Ruckles had magically appeared to pull out the chairs for their guests. Sam seated the two women on his left and right, then waited for some kind of signal from Elizabeth.

"The room was created in the 1780s, when it was fashionable to entertain small groups of people," Elizabeth said. "I hope you will enjoy dining in here."

"How old is the tapestry, Lord Longford?"

"Please, call me Sam." He ignored the woman's look of surprise and raised his voice. "Darling, we have a question about the tapestry. Would you like to tell us about it?" He turned back to his guest. "Elizabeth is the expert in the family. I, uh, spend a lot of time outdoors."

Elizabeth told the history of the tapestry—a hideous carpet with pudgy cherubs and constipated-looking knights—while Pattie and Peggie served bowls of steaming onion soup and placed silver baskets piled high with rolls. Elizabeth had a knack for making history sound fascinating, but Sam had seen enough ancient tapestries in the past week to carpet Yankee Stadium.

He lifted a bottle from its nearby stand. "Wine, anyone?"

"I CAN'T BELIEVE you kept pouring drinks," Elizabeth sputtered. "As if my guests were in the local pub."

"I was trying to be hospitable," Sam said, following her down a long hallway. "No one complained. The ladies were very pleased with the attention."

"They were *drunk*." The long dress kept her from moving as fast as she would have liked, and she wished the new "lord" Longford would go to bed and stop talking to her.

"Not all of them." Sam opened a thick door for her when she would have done it herself. "A couple of the older ladies, Ellen and Marje, I think, were just fine."

"Not really." She'd seen them wobbling off to bed, supporting each other up the wide staircase. "You're not the one who has to worry about lawsuits."

"Maybe it was jet lag."

"Maybe it was the brandy you gave them."

"I didn't exactly pour it down their throats. Where the hell are we going? This place smells like a dungeon."

He was right, she knew. The stone passageway always smelled damp. "To the kitchen. Watch this puddle."

Too late. He splashed water along the hem of her dress. "Sorry."

"Drat."

"I've never heard anyone say *drat* before. I thought that went out with Dickens."

And now he was criticizing her language. Would this day never end? Elizabeth paused in front of the kitchen door. "Good night, Mr. Martin. If you turn around and go back the way you came, you'll find the staircase soon enough."

"Look," he said, refusing to budge. "I was just trying to be a good host. They ate and drank everything that was put in front of them. Ruckles disappeared, so—"

"He didn't disappear. I sent him to bed." She turned on a light to reveal a large, yellow kitchen. "These long days are difficult for him."

"And you?"

"I have dishes to clean." She grabbed an apron from a hook by the door and tugged it over her head.

"Don't you have help for jobs like that?"

"Up to a point. The girls cleaned most of the mess, but I don't expect them to work from eight in the morning until midnight." Elizabeth surveyed the kitchen. An array of cups, saucers and small plates littered the counter by the sink, but to her relief everything else had been cleaned and put away.

"I thought you would have a staff of ten or twenty people." He leaned against the counter and crossed his arms in front of his chest.

"In my grandmother's day, yes, that would be true." She turned on the water and began to fill up the sink with water.

"Don't you have a dishwasher?"

She slipped on a pair of rubber gloves and squirted dish soap under the running water. "Of course, but these gold-edged dishes need to be washed by hand."

He moved away, took off his jacket and draped it over a chair. "You want me to dry?"

"You're volunteering to help?"

"Don't look so surprised. Just because I didn't volunteer to be your husband doesn't mean I don't dry dishes." Sam rolled up his sleeves.

She tossed him a towel and turned back to the sink. "I'd be happy for the help." She would be happier if he'd leave and go to bed. She didn't like the way he made her feel—like a sixteen-year-old, stammering in front of the star of the rugby team. And stammer she had, those years ago, when she was shy and chubby and wore braces on her teeth.

Elizabeth banished the memory and attacked the china. She washed and rinsed the delicate teacups, while Sam dried them with quick motions and stacked them in alarmingly casual heaps.

"Surely it's obvious that this isn't going to work," he said after a long silence.

"What do you mean?"

"I mean, I'll take my mother out of here in the morning. You can say that Lord Longford and his mother have been called away. An emergency. Everyone already knows that she isn't feeling well."

Elizabeth knew she should agree. He'd gotten her guests more than a little inebriated. His accent was clearly American. He knew nothing about Longley and even less about entertaining ten businesswomen. He was a stranger; she knew nothing about him except he was kind to his mother, could wield a dish towel and had the sexiest smile she'd ever seen.

Somehow all three of those qualities seemed terribly important.

"We had an agreement," she reminded him. "And your mother is very happily settled in the blue bedroom, even though she isn't feeling well."

"My mother has a way of creating adventures wherever she goes."

"You think she's pretending to be ill?"

"No. I saw her turn pale. It was pretty frightening." He leaned against the counter and shot her a rueful smile. "But how did she go from crashing to the floor to sleeping in some ancient bed while her son wears tight pants and cleans up the kitchen?"

Elizabeth had to laugh. The American looked so frustrated. "Your mother is quite lovely. Let her stay in her bed and rest. Perhaps the tour was too strenuous, and she'll be herself with a day or two of rest. Of course, if she is really ill, we can call a doctor immediately." She handed him another dripping teacup. "Besides, the ladies adored you."

The idiot looked surprised. Then pleased. "Really?"

She nodded. "Yes. Your complete lack of historical knowledge somehow charmed them into thinking you have more important things on your mind."

"Like what?"

"I don't know, but I overheard two of them whispering that they thought you must spend a lot of time overseas on business. I think that was after you 'forgot' where the library was located."

"Oh. Sorry about that."

"I'll see that you receive a map," she promised. "I had some drawn up for the weekend."

"Good idea. This place must have three hundred rooms."

"The estate is enormous, but we use only a fraction of the rooms. That should make it somewhat easier."

"Where are all these women sleeping?"

She handed him a large platter. "Some are on the ground floor. Others are on the first floor, or second floor as you Americans prefer to call it. All the public rooms you saw today are on that upper floor. There's another story, too, but we may never restore those rooms. We have piles of furniture and paintings upstairs that could take me a lifetime to catalogue."

"A lifetime," he repeated, swiping the cloth across the plate. "You certainly are devoted."

"You make that sound like something awful."

He gave her an odd look. "You're very young to devote yourself to a house. Don't you have a life of your own?"

Ouch. He'd hit a very large, very painful spot. Elizabeth turned away and dumped another stack of dirty plates into the sink. "That really isn't any of your business."

"I'm your husband," the man had the nerve to tease. "I should know these things."

"You don't—" pain sliced through her left index finger and made her gasp "—know anything. Oh, for heaven's sake, that hurt."

"I was just teasing," he said, peering at her face. "You don't have to cry."

Elizabeth blinked back the tears. "I'm not crying. I cut my finger and it stings a bit." She pulled her hands out of the water to show him. "I must have broken a dish."

"You should get rid of all of these old things and start over," he said, helping her take the glove from her hand. Blood ran from the gash in her finger, so he turned on the water and put her hand underneath it.

"These 'old things' are valuable antiques."

"They're also dangerous. How's that?"

"Better." The cold water began to numb the cut nicely. She managed a smile, though she felt ridiculous. With her free hand she reached for the roll of paper towels that hung nearby.

"I'll get that." And he did, wrapping her dripping hand with gentle and quick motions.

"Do you have children?"

"No." He gave her a questioning look. "Why?"

Elizabeth tried to explain without saying that his gentle touch had been appreciated. "You handle little emergencies very well."

"I spent three years as a camp counselor. Where do you keep the Band-Aids?"

"There's a medical kit in the cupboard in the china pantry."

He frowned. "You want to point me in that direction?"

"I'll get it." She moved away from him before he had a chance to argue. There was no easy way to explain which cupboard or which pantry, and besides, he'd been standing too close.

Elizabeth returned with the box of first aid supplies and set it on the counter. The bleeding had slowed, though the paper was soaked with blood, and her finger still throbbed. Sam rummaged through the box until he found the box of large Band-Aids, then he peeled back the paper towel and applied the bandage to her finger.

"There," he said, holding her hand so her fingers were raised. "I don't think it's bad enough to need stitches."

"I'm sure it's not," she agreed. "I should have been more careful."

He glanced toward the soapy water in the sink. "Accidents happen. I'll find that broken dish and get it out of there."

"Thank you." He took his hand from hers, which was probably a pretty good idea. She had begun to like having her hand held.

Within minutes he'd drained the water from the sink, collected the broken pieces of a saucer and rinsed the rest of the dishes. He left them on a dish towel and surveyed the rest of the kitchen, before turning back to her.

"Can we go to bed now?" he asked, drying his hands.

"Excuse me?"

His expression didn't change as he tossed the towel onto the counter. "The lord of the manor has no idea how to get back to his bedroom."

"I'll take you. Ruckles put you in the east wing, near the family's private rooms." In the room where Anthony the Rat should have been sleeping.

Sam shrugged. "I don't know if that's up or down, left or right. Tomorrow I'll use bread crumbs."

"I won't forget about that map." She had no business being attracted to him, she reminded herself once again. But she was human. And he was gorgeous. And they were both young and single and standing alone together late at night in her kitchen. And kitchens could be romantic. She'd seen the movie *Bull Durham,* where the hero had swept the dishes from the tabletop and made love to the heroine right then and there. She'd envied that kind of passion.

It was one of her favorite movies.

"Elizabeth?" Sam stopped near the door. "Are you okay?"

"I'm fine," she assured him, turning out the lights and trying to remember that Sam was a guest in her home. "Breakfast will be available from seven to eleven. You can come to the dining room anytime you like.''

"If I can find it," he grumbled.

She led him back into the dim passageway and shut the door behind them. "I guess you'll just have to follow the smell of sausage."

"You're going to feed sausage to ten women with hangovers?"

"Watch the puddle."

He stepped sideways and landed on the hem of her dress, knocking her against the wall. His arms came around to balance them both, his large body leaning against hers as Elizabeth was backed against the wall. She held on to him to keep from falling.

"Are you okay?"

"You keep asking me that question. I'm fine. Perhaps you'd take your foot off my dress?"

He moved his feet, but his arms stayed around her. She supposed he was afraid she would topple over if he let go. "Do you have other dresses, or have I ruined the only one?"

"I have a few more," she whispered, wondering why she was so warm. The wall behind her was cool, but the parts of her touching Sam Martin were growing more heated by the second.

"Should I let go or will you fall?" His voice was low, his lips dangerously close to hers as he bent to look into her face.

"I won't fall," she promised, but he moved his hands to her shoulders and brushed her lips with his.

"Nice," he whispered.

"You sound surprised."

"I am." He touched her lips again, this time applying more pressure.

"Why?" she managed to ask. "Haven't you kissed an English lady before?"

"I've kissed a lot of ladies," he said with a chuckle in his voice. He backed up to release her. "But not in England." He took her hand from his waist and his gaze dropped to her chest. "I told you they were going to fall out."

"THERE ARE MORE where that came from," Ruckles declared, shaking the dust from his hands. With his foot, he pushed the heavy trunk toward the bed. "There is no chronological order, of course, which is a pity."

"Yes," Betsy agreed, eyeing the trunk. She wasn't sure she felt like doing Longley research at six o'clock in the morning, but she'd been awake since five making plans for her future. It was hard to make plans on an empty stomach, and she didn't dare go roaming around the house looking for a coffee pot and a toaster. She didn't doubt her son's intention of getting on a plane as soon as humanly possible, and that's exactly what would happen if Sam found out she was feeling better. "What exactly do you want me to look for?"

"Anything that describes furniture purchased or made in the 1500s," he said, looking down his long nose at her. "And, of course, anything that pertains to a visit made by Queen Elizabeth to Longley."

Betsy brightened. "I could prove she slept in this bed then?"

"It's possible," he conceded with a sniff. "But highly unlikely. Still, the publicity would help Longley's tourist business. Lady Elizabeth would certainly be pleased."

"I see." Pleasing Lady Elizabeth would be an excellent beginning, Betsy decided. Miserable young women did not fall in love as easily as happy young women. Not that it was difficult to fall in love with Samuel, but Lord knew that young man needed all the help he could get in *that* department.

Ruckles knelt on the carpet and lifted the lid of the trunk as Betsy leaned over to peer inside. Stacks of papers and leather-bound notebooks filled the trunk. Betsy sneezed as the butler handed her one of the bundles of letters. "Elizabeth won't mind my reading these?"

"I doubt it, madam. She's given me leave to examine the family's papers. A historically accurate account of her ancestors would be something her visitors might expect to purchase." The butler puffed with pride at the announcement.

"And you would be the author of such a book?"

"Of course. Who else?" He stood up and brushed imaginary bits of dust from his dark pants. "I will mention your help in the preface, naturally."

"Naturally." She untied the faded blue ribbon, and the letters fell into her lap. "I wonder what I'll find in here."

"Concentrate on furniture and the queen," he reminded her. "I will fill in the other centuries as I go along."

"I'm a fast reader. And I'll take notes."

"Excellent," the butler stated. "I'll leave you to it, then."

"Wait a minute," she called. "What about breakfast?"

He looked surprised as he backed toward the door. "Breakfast will be served in the dining room between the hours of seven and eleven."

"I'm supposed to be sick, remember?"

The man nodded, his expression serious. "Yes, madam. I will see that the maid brings a tray."

"Thank you." Betsy paused. "Wait a minute, Ruckles. You haven't told me how last night went."

He hesitated as he opened the door. "Last night?"

"My son. How did he do?"

"He was...adequate, madam." With that grim adjective, Ruckles opened the door and swept out of the room. The door shut behind him with a dull click, and Betsy was left alone to shake the dust from ancient papers and to contemplate how good a cup of coffee was going to taste.

Adequate. Sam overheard the description of his performance as he stood in the hall. It had taken him ten minutes and three dead ends before he'd rediscovered his mother's whereabouts. Pattie or Peggie had pointed him in this direction and wished him good-morning.

Ruckles nodded as he passed him in the hall. "Good morning, sir."

"Good morning."

"Your mother is awake," the man informed him.

"Yes. I heard. I came to see how she is feeling."

The man hesitated. "I'm sure she will be happy to tell you herself."

Sam hid a smile. "Really?" The butler remained impassive. "Is there anything special happening this morning?" He hoped not. He would like to explore some of the countryside and find a *New York Times*. He would like to call the office and see what crises had erupted in the past few days. He would like to reserve rooms at a hotel next to Heathrow and book a flight home.

The butler didn't bother to hide his dismay. "You didn't receive a schedule?"

"No." He should have known there would be a schedule. After all, the British had attempted to organize most of the world at one time.

"I will see that one is delivered to your room."

"No hurry. I can wait to find out what Lady Liz has planned for me."

With that he broke into a whistle and knocked on his mother's door twice before entering the room. Bright with morning light, the blue bedroom was cheerier than he remembered it from yesterday. His mother sat in a nest of pillows, her lap covered with papers and her reading glasses perched on her nose. "Mother? What are you doing?"

"A little research, dear." She put down the papers she was reading and smiled at him. "Nothing strenuous."

"How are you feeling?" To his relief, he saw that she wore makeup and lipstick, and her short gray hair was in its usual styled waves. "I see that you've been up and around."

"A little. And I'm feeling a bit better."

"Well enough to leave here?"

She ignored the question and put the papers in neat stacks. "How was your evening last night?"

Sam had to struggle to answer. How was he supposed to describe stepping on Lady Lizzie's dress, or kissing those very soft lips or...the effect a glance at those lovely bare breasts had had on him. "It was fine."

"Fine. Adequate. Hmm..." She gave him an amused look and climbed to her feet. "I can't wait to find out what our hostess says."

"Maybe you shouldn't ask her."

"Did the ladies believe you were married? Was she happy with the dinner? She must have said *something* to you about the way the evening went."

"Aside from telling me to go to the devil?"

"Quit teasing, Sam."

He wasn't teasing. The lady had pulled her bodice over her breasts and stalked toward the door. She had wished him to the devil, led him silently throughout the house, pointed out his door and told him she hoped he would be gone in the morning.

"She loved me," Sam told his mother. "She couldn't be more pleased with the whole arrangement."

"Of course she is. Why wouldn't she be?"

Sam could think of a few reasons. "Tell me you're well enough to leave this place once and for all," he said, sitting on the edge of the bed.

"Be careful," she cautioned, moving the papers and envelopes out of his way. "These are very old."

He picked up one of the envelopes, noticing the faded writing and, on the back, the broken seal of wax. "What are you doing with these?"

"Entertaining myself."

He tossed the envelope back onto the pile. "There are plenty of ways to entertain yourself at home, Mother."

She gave him a stern look. "I have three days of vacation left, Sam. Don't spoil it."

"Spoil it?" He couldn't help laughing. "I'm worried about your health. I think you should see a doctor. I think we should go home."

She shook an envelope at him. "Don't start trying to boss me around, Samuel. I'm still your mother and I don't have to listen to you."

Which, of course, was the problem.

5

"OH, MADAM, you mustn't!"

Elizabeth repeated her instructions to the horrified butler. "Pack his things and see that he is taken to the inn in town."

Ruckles didn't move from his place at the foot of the main staircase. If she didn't know better, she'd think the man was disappointed. He cleared his throat. "And what is to be done with *Mrs.* Martin?"

"She shall stay here until Monday morning, as we agreed." No matter how upset she was, Elizabeth couldn't toss that sweet, elderly woman out of the blue bedroom.

"And may I inquire what we should tell our guests as to Lord Longford's whereabouts?"

"I'll think of something," she assured him. "He'll go to London. An emergency. An illness of a relative. A business crisis."

Ruckles looked ready to weep. "Business? What shall I say is Lord Longford's occupation?"

"Food," came the answer. Only the voice was low

and amused and completely male. Elizabeth turned around to see Sam Martin standing behind her.

"Haven't you found the dining room yet?" She glanced down to make sure her blouse was buttoned and tucked securely into the waistband of her wool slacks. The movement was not lost to her "guest." He smiled that gorgeous, sexy smile and melted Elizabeth's knees.

"You're not in costume this morning," he said.

"I learned it wasn't practical." She lifted her chin in the air. "You're eavesdropping again, I see."

He shrugged. "Sound carries on these marble floors. You're not afraid your guests are listening?"

"No one is awake yet." She looked at her watch. "Breakfast won't be ready for another ten minutes." She had a thousand things to do, and instead here she stood, wasting precious time sparring with the American. The American who had kissed her and glimpsed her breasts.

"So you are going to send me away?"

"Please lower your voice." Elizabeth saw Ruckles move away from them. "Yes. I definitely think it would be best if you leave. I never should have believed this was possible in the first place."

He didn't seem upset with the news. "I wasn't a good enough lord?"

"You just won't do," she fibbed. He was all easy charm and nice manners and disarming American frankness. He was broad shoulders and warm lips and brown eyes that twinkled with good humor.

"And if I refuse to go?"

He was also a royal pain. "I will call the constable."

His eyebrows rose. "Really? How entertaining for the travel agents." Sam smiled, just a little. "You're bluffing, Lady Liz." He leaned closer and whispered, "Are you still upset about that kiss?"

"I'm a little old to be upset by something so…trivial." There. She waited for him to stomp off and pack his suitcase.

"That's true. How old *are* you?"

"That's none of your business."

"Thirty? Women start getting sensitive about their age about that time of—"

"Twenty-eight."

"Okay. Twenty-eight. And I'm not leaving, as much as I'd like to."

"Oh, for heaven's sake," she hissed, trying to keep her temper. "This whole thing is ridiculous, and you and I both know it."

"And you and I both know that my mother is in that ugly old bed upstairs, so it's not that simple."

"She can stay. You can't."

"I'm not leaving her here with strangers. I'm staying right here, if I have to pretend to be your husband or not. You agreed to this, my mother is happy, and

I'm going to see that she stays that way. At least she's getting some rest. Write up a bill, I'll give you my credit card, and I will become plain Sam Martin the guest, until my mother is well enough to leave.''

"I can't tell those women that you're not my husband. How would it look if they realized I—''

A scream, followed by a loud crash, stopped her words, and the three of them looked toward the top of the stairs. Barbara Canfield peered over the banister. "It's all right, folks. The maid dropped a tray, that's all.''

"Is she hurt?''

Pattie's flushed face appeared above the railing. "Not a bit, m'lady. I'm very sorry. I think I tripped over my own feet. Mrs. Martin's breakfast—''

"Will be taken care of,'' Elizabeth called, then realized to her embarrassment that she was shouting, as several other heads appeared near Pattie's. Some of her guests were awake. There would be no more discussions with Sam for a while, at least not downstairs. There was some good-natured laughter mingling with the sound of china. Elizabeth moved toward the stairs. "I'll be right there.''

"I'll go help with the cleaning up,'' Sam offered, moving ahead of her. "We don't want any accidents like last night.''

"And I'll fix another tray for your mother.'' She turned to the butler. "Ruckles, would you make certain the other ladies know that breakfast is available downstairs at their convenience?''

He didn't bother to hide his sigh. ''Of course.''

Elizabeth watched as he moved slowly toward the staircase. Sam turned and called, ''Ruckles, never mind. I'll tell them.''

''Yes, m'lord.''

''Darling?''

Elizabeth, aware of the audience peering over the banister, tried to look loving. Which wasn't easy, despite how good Sam looked in his well-worn jeans. She hardened her heart and other parts of her anatomy. ''What?''

''You will be joining me for breakfast, I hope?''

''I have to—''

He smiled. ''Good. We need to discuss the plans for the day.''

She decided against arguing with him. They'd discuss the plans, all right. Those plans would include how to get rid of Lord Longford. She would be glad to see the last of him. After all, she didn't need to be distracted by unnecessary physical attraction. She turned to Ruckles and caught his eye.

''Do it,'' she mouthed silently.

The butler nodded, but his back straightened in unspoken disapproval.

''THEY'RE FIGHTING.''

Betsy climbed out of the bed and bounced on her

toes. She did a couple of deep knee bends and then stretched her fingers toward the ceiling. "Of course they are. It's called 'sexual tension.'"

Ruckles snorted, and the tip of his nose turned pink. "Mrs. Martin, really!"

"Yes," she said, shaking her arms at her sides. "Really. It's in all of the books I've read. *Sexual tension.* It means they're very attracted to each other."

"It does?"

"From the minute they saw each other, I knew it was meant to be. The fortune-teller told me, you know. She said I would meet my destiny in a blue bedroom in a golden house. And she said there would be many changes, but they would be good ones. For both my son and myself."

"Lady E. is supposedly one of the changes?"

Betsy nodded and walked over to the chair. She had moved it by the window so she could look outside and admire her new home. "She's the best one. She's a lovely girl. Very kind. She'll make a wonderful mother for my granddaughters."

The butler gulped. "Children? I never thought—"

Betsy realized she'd made a tactical error. "Oh," she said, waving her arm as if dismissing the thought of pretty little Martin girls. "That would be years and years away."

"And they will have nannies, of course."

"Of course." Over her dead body. "But first, we have to see that Sam and Elizabeth are forced to be together."

"She has told me to pack his suitcase and drive him to town."

"And have you done it?"

"No. I came up here to tell you. They're expecting me downstairs for the rest of the morning. I'm to help serve breakfast, then I'm to escort lost tourists from room to room." He sighed as if tortured. "No one respects a writer's time."

"I do," Betsy said, making soothing noises. "I know how important it is for you to write. That's why it will be so nice for you when Sam is doing all of the work around here. You'll have time for your research." She picked up a stack of letters and placed them on her lap. "I'm enjoying these, you know."

He sighed again. "You'll have to return to bed. Someone will be bringing your breakfast tray at any moment."

Betsy stood and carried the papers to the bed. Once she was settled under the faded blue covers, her pillows propped nicely against her back, she picked up the stack of letters. "There. All set for a nice day here on the estate."

"I trust you'll call me immediately if you find anything of interest?"

"Immediately," Betsy promised.

"Madam?" He still didn't move toward the door.

"Yes?"

"What should I do about your son's suitcase?"

Betsy looked up and smiled. "Don't do a thing. Not yet. Sam isn't going to leave me. And he is too nice a man to have done anything to upset Elizabeth."

"Lady E. has scolded him."

"Sexual tension, remember?"

Another horrified look crossed the butler's face. "If you say so, madam, but—"

"Worry about nothing," she told him, waving one hand toward the door. "Have your breakfast and guide your guests. I'll take care of my son."

Ruckles looked as if he wanted to protest, but then changed his mind as he saw the papers in her hand. He needed help, she knew. In more ways than one.

Everyone's prayers had been answered. They just didn't know it yet.

"IT'S LIKE there was something there," Pattie insisted, her eyes wide. "The strangest thing I've ever felt."

"Something there?" Elizabeth stopped spooning sausages onto Mrs. Martin's breakfast plate. "Whatever are you talking about?"

"I don't know, m'lady. I couldn't see anything in

front of me, then quick as a wink I bumped into...someone.''

"An invisible someone.''

"Yes, m'lady.'' Pattie winced. "I was up half the night with the baby. Maybe I didn't get enough rest.''

Elizabeth relaxed a little and resumed her job assembling another breakfast. A young mother's sleepless night could easily explain what happened upstairs. "Go home early today. Peggie and I will manage without you this afternoon.''

"It's getting better. Johnny says he'll take over tonight so I can get more rest. He doesn't have to get up for work tomorrow.''

"Go home and take a nap,'' Elizabeth insisted. "I'll be busy with the guests all afternoon. I'm taking them for a drive around the countryside.''

"They'll love that, m'lady. And you need to leave the house for a while, too.''

Elizabeth put the plate on a tray, added juice, a fresh pot of tea and a plate of toast. "What do you mean?''

The girl blushed. "A bit of fresh air would do you good, put some color in your cheeks. You shouldn't be in the kitchen all day.'' She giggled. "He's a handsome man, m'lady.'' They both knew she wasn't talking about the butler. "Those American men are very tempting, they are. And you spend too much time alone here in Longley. It might be time to have some fun for yourself.''

''I don't think Mr. Martin is 'fun,' Pattie.''

The maid winked. ''He's the kind of man a woman wouldn't mind having in her bed for a *little* while at least.''

''Pattie!'' Elizabeth turned back to the eggs that were due to be stirred. ''For heaven's sake.''

Pattie picked up the tray. ''You'll never marry again if you stay cooped up here, that's all.'' She headed toward the doorway. ''I'll try again, m'lady. Only this time I'm saying my prayers. There's some odd things going on upstairs.''

Elizabeth opened her mouth to protest, then thought better of it. There were lots of odd things going on: a woman fainting in the blue bedroom, an aggravating American pretending to be Lord Longford, maids tripping over things that weren't there...

And her unexplainable attraction to Sam Martin.

Which was going to end *now*. Surely she could manage to avoid him for the rest of the day.

''DARLING, what did you do to your finger?'' Sam bent down and gave Elizabeth a quick kiss on the cheek, patted her shoulder and said his greetings to the three women eating breakfast. Instead of walking to the other end of the long table, he took a seat near Elizabeth and beside a guest.

"That looks painful," Melissa Lee said, eyeing the large bandage. Elizabeth hesitated and Sam lifted his cup so Peggie could fill it with coffee.

"Thanks," he said, watching his "wife." Would the lady admit she had been washing dishes at midnight? He didn't think so.

"I cut myself in the garden this morning," she admitted.

"You should be more careful, sweetheart," Sam said, taking a sip of the worst coffee he had ever tasted in his life. "Let the gardener do those things."

"I will from now on."

"The flowers are lovely," Phyllis said. "I really enjoyed walking through the gardens yesterday."

"They're not the size they were in my grandmother's time," Elizabeth said in her most ladylike voice, "but we're slowly returning them to their former condition."

He wondered who *we* was exactly. He'd bet his last dollar that Elizabeth had had her hands on a shovel this past summer. This woman would work right alongside the gardener and not think twice.

"How long have you lived here, Lady Elizabeth?" another early-morning riser asked.

"Please, call me Liz. Or Elizabeth." She smiled. Sam drew in his breath. She was such a lovely woman, especially when she wore that fluffy hair loose, down to her shoulders.

"Darling, what are the plans for the day? I'm afraid I haven't seen the schedule yet," Sam said, taking a sip of coffee. "Do you need me for anything in particular?"

"If anyone is interested in seeing some of the countryside, I'd be happy to take them on a drive. Jane Austen once lived in this neighborhood, remember?"

"Jane *who?*" He deliberately looked puzzled.

"Austen," she repeated, then she smiled at the lady on her right. "Sam isn't much of a reader," she said, keeping her tone light. Still, he didn't miss the glint in her eyes.

"I read," he protested. "I treasure my copies of *Sports Illustrated,*" he confided to the woman on his left. "I'm a big football fan. Those years in the States, you know."

"Don't you want to help yourself to some breakfast?" Elizabeth asked.

"In a minute." He winced when he took another sip of coffee. "One of these days I'll get used to the British version of coffee."

"Anyway," Elizabeth said, ignoring him, "we're planning an outing for those who wish to see some of the area. It's a lovely day to explore."

"Then you don't need me," he said, not bothering to hide his satisfaction.

"No. We don't, dearest. You're free to putter in the gardens until teatime."

"That's what English gentlemen do best," he said, standing up and approaching the sideboard. Sunlight streamed in from the long windows and made the silver shine. He piled an array of food on a gilt-edged, washed-and-dried-by-hand plate, grabbed one of the newspapers from the basket and returned to the table. He winked at Elizabeth, which made her blush, then reached for the paper as the ladies excused themselves.

Elizabeth stayed, despite his deliberately noisy table manners. He wanted her to leave. He was a person who enjoyed reading and eating at the same time.

"You're not fooling me," she said.

"The prime minister is meeting with the queen today to discuss world trade agreements."

"I don't want to see you until teatime."

"There was another bombing in Covent Garden." He put down the paper. "What time is tea?"

"Three o'clock."

"Fine."

She leaned forward and whispered, "Stay out of my way."

He tilted her chin with one finger and kissed her before she could realize what he was going to do. She tasted of peppermint tea, and her lips were as soft and inviting as they had been last night.

"If you don't stop that, I'll—"

"Darling," he warned, seeing a flash of color by the door. "We don't have time for this now. Let me eat my breakfast."

"Lady Elizabeth?" Phyllis called. "Is it all right if I take a walk before breakfast?"

Elizabeth leaned closer and kept her voice low as she whispered in his ear, "Touch me again and I'll fry your little body parts for dinner." Then she turned and smiled at her guest. "Of course you may walk anywhere you like. Breakfast is here whenever you are ready for it. Do you have a map of the grounds?"

"They're not little," he protested, but Elizabeth didn't turn around.

She scurried off to make sure the woman wouldn't get lost, and Sam was left to a quiet dining room and a newspaper full of information he didn't care to read. Elizabeth kissed like an angel. Despite her protests, they both knew that she'd kissed him back. And that made her angry.

And made him chuckle.

Sam didn't know why he enjoyed teasing her so much. Maybe because she was so serious about everything, so intent on making certain everything was perfect for her guests. He didn't understand why she went through so much trouble. Surely she could sell the place and live like a queen elsewhere. One of the hall paintings looked like a Rubens. And he would have sworn there was an authentic Rodin sculpture in the center of that cold black-and-white tiled hall. Lady Elizabeth could have one hell of a yard sale and set herself up someplace where there weren't any puddles on the way to the kitchen.

It wasn't right that a woman like her stayed cooped up in an old ruin. But if she was crazy it was none of his business.

He'd be gone as soon as he could get his mother out of that musty old bed, and not a minute later. It was time for someone around here to show some sense.

"AFTER TEA I'll show you the rest of the original part of the house," Elizabeth promised her guests. She'd thought to liven things up by serving tea in the old kitchen. The medieval room, with its vaulted ceiling and soot-covered stone walls, boasted an assortment of elk heads and turtle shells and was always popular with the day visitors.

"Turtle shells?" Marje-from-Phoenix asked. "Really?"

"For the turtle soup." Elizabeth pointed out the turtle-shaped tureen sitting on top of one of the large black stoves. "I think my ancestors cooked up quite a bit of it."

"Do you use this room for cooking?"

"No. We have a more modern addition on the west wing," Elizabeth assured her. "But it's lovely to see how our ancestors prepared food four hundred years ago."

The ladies agreed, and the silver-haired Ms. Canfield wrote something down in a notebook. Melissa Lee cocked her head. "Does anyone hear something?"

The clanking of teacups stopped as the ladies listened. Somewhere someone sang "God Bless America" in a boisterous, off-key baritone.

"It's so nice to have a man around," one of the women pointed out. "My Robert used to sing like that."

"He's singing a patriotic American song," was Nancy Mack's comment. "Isn't that sweet?"

Sweet? She didn't think that was the adjective she would use. Elizabeth peered toward the ceiling. Sam couldn't possibly be in that section of the house. No one had been up there in years. But then again, the sound of singing was coming from up above. Unless Ruckles had discovered the virtues of American music, Sam was in the old apartments.

He was doing this to annoy her, of course. She had told him she didn't want to see him until teatime, so he had made certain she and the ladies would *hear* him instead.

And he couldn't even sing. Elizabeth reached for

the teapot and began to refill her guest's cups. "Lord Longford is very...musical. He is quite good at entertaining himself, too, and—"

"'My home, sweet...*home!*'"

A large chunk of plaster fell from the ceiling and knocked the turtle-shaped tureen onto the floor, where it shattered into pieces. The women, safely away from the stove to begin with, scattered to the other end of the kitchen. Dorla screamed. Barbara Canfield swore.

And everyone looked up at the ceiling as the dust filtered down from an octagonal hole where a man's bare legs dangled sixteen feet in the air.

The singing had stopped.

The cursing had begun.

6

"SAM!" Elizabeth cupped her hands around her mouth and raised her voice. "Are you hurt?"

The cursing stopped. "Lizzie? Where are you?"

"Below you, in the old kitchen. Are you hurt?" she asked again.

"Not yet, but I'm stuck in this damn hole!"

She turned back to her guests. "Ladies, I think it would be best if you left the kitchen while I see to...Lord Longford. Is anyone hurt?"

The women shook their heads. A few had plaster dust in their hair, but most were still holding their teacups.

Ms. Lee eyed Sam's legs. "What can we do to help?"

"Get me out of here," he yelled.

Elizabeth answered as calmly as she could. "If you could find the butler and send him to the old apartments, that would be lovely," she said, hurrying out of the room. She took the back staircase and, instead of turning into the public rooms, rushed the opposite way toward the other wing.

It didn't take long to find him once she crossed the hall and circled back around to the unused rooms above the kitchen. She followed the sound of muttered curses through a set of apartments that hadn't been used for thirty years.

"Sam?" She ran towards the bathroom. "What on earth—"

"It's simple," he said through gritted teeth. "I've fallen through your rotting sixteenth-century floor. Don't come any closer or we could both go through."

"Are you sure you're not hurt?" He was naked. Gloriously naked, from what she could see. His hair was wet, dripping onto those incredible shoulders. He had that broad, bare back to her, so she didn't feel quite so awkward approaching him. Backs were a lot safer to look at than fronts.

"I don't think so, but something is digging into my…thigh and I don't want to make any sudden moves, if you know what I mean."

She knew what he meant. She got down on her hands and knees and crawled closer. "Let me see."

"Let you see? No way."

"Or we could wait for Ruckles."

That didn't seem to appeal to him, either. "In that case, I'll be here until dark."

"I'm your only hope. And I'm not going to be overcome with lust at the sight of a naked man," she promised, moving closer. There was no blood, most of Sam was supported by the bathroom floor, and he was well enough to argue with her. Good signs.

"I'm not talking about lust. This morning you were threatening mutilation. I'm not taking any chances," he muttered. "Stop where you are." He groped for a bath towel and draped it around himself as she inched toward him.

"I was married once," she reminded him. "Isn't there an expression, 'If you've seen one you've seen them all'?"

He opened his mouth and, as if changing his mind about responding, closed it again. "You're not seeing this one, lady. The last time we talked you threatened to unman me." He looked down at the place where his thighs were encased in flooring. "Looks like this damn house has done it for you."

"Oh, stop complaining," she said, peering down into the hole. "You've fallen through that odd-shaped part of the kitchen ceiling. I wonder what this used to be."

"Could we talk about history after I'm out of here?"

"Right or left? Which is stuck?"

"Right."

She leaned over his lap and carefully reached down along his right thigh. His firm, large, warm right thigh. She was more than a little conscious of the position she was in. A few more centimeters and her cheek would be touching that towel. Her fingers touched a chunk of plaster. "Got it," she announced.

"Got what?"

She moved forward a little more and wiggled the chunk. "Plaster. And I don't feel any blood. Are you in pain?"

"Ow!"

She stopped and turned to look up at him. "That hurts?"

"Your elbow," he said, moving her arm away from his crotch. "You are trying to castrate me, aren't you?"

"Sorry." She turned back to her work. "It's not rotten wood. It's plaster. Someone must have plastered over the hole at one time," she murmured, feeling carefully to make sure there were no nails or large splinters of wood. "It was most likely a lantern hole, due to the odd shape. And you're the first one to jump through it."

"I didn't 'jump.' I merely stepped out of the shower. A *lukewarm* shower."

"And into the old kitchen. The guests were a bit surprised."

"Yeah, well, they weren't the only ones. I thought I was going to plunge to my death." In less than a minute, Elizabeth had pried the plaster loose. They heard it crash onto the rest of the broken crockery.

Elizabeth sat up and Sam pulled his legs out of the hole. He fell backward, taking Elizabeth with him away from further trouble.

"Your towel—"

"It's here some—"

"Lady Elizabeth, you were asking for me?" Ruckles stood in the doorway, disapproval written all over his long face as he surveyed the scene before him. Clearly he was not pleased with the sight of his employer half-sprawled over a naked guest.

"Yes," she managed to say, though Sam's hand was on her derriere. She tried not to envision how much of Sam's body was exposed. "We have a bit of a problem with the ceiling."

"I see. I will make certain the doors are kept locked."

"Thank you, Ruckles. I would appreciate it if you would have fresh tea set up in the library for our guests."

He nodded. "Will there be anything else, m'lady?"

"Not at the moment, thank you."

Ruckles closed the door on his way out.

"Would you remove your hand from my...body, please?"

He kissed her first, which was easily done because she was inches from his face and didn't even make an attempt to stop him. Elizabeth should have been surprised, but she wasn't. Even when he parted her lips with his tongue and deepened the kiss, she accepted it as an inevitable result of touching him, of kissing him, of being in the same room with him. For some odd reason every time they were together she thought about sex.

This time it was Sam who stopped first. He removed his hand and lifted her away from him. "Sorry. I used you to cover myself. No telling who was coming in."

"Next time use a towel," she said, scrambling to her feet without looking at him. "Next time take a shower in your own bathroom."

"There wasn't a shower. Just a bathtub."

She brushed plaster dust from her jeans. "Then take a bath."

"I don't like baths, but I'll learn. And from now on I'll watch where I step around here. This old place is dangerous," he said, groaning as he stood up. "I'm damn lucky I escaped with my manhood."

"And I'm lucky your 'manhood' wasn't exposed to the ladies downstairs." Elizabeth closed her eyes in a brief prayer of thanks to the gods of tourism.

"Where the hell are my clothes?"

Elizabeth opened her eyes and saw the neat pile of clothing stacked beside the sink. She scooped it up and tossed it to him. He caught it as she realized he had been standing there naked.

She turned away and headed for the door. He was trying to make her crazy. She knew he was. It was part of some master plan to destroy her business—what there was of it—and annihilate Longley, a building that had stood valiantly since the year 1515.

"Don't you want to know how the Lord Longford spent his day?"

She kept walking. "I don't think I want to."

She heard him chuckle. "All right. I'll wait for you to notice."

Elizabeth grabbed the doorknob and kept right on moving. "Thank you, Mr. Martin, but I'm certain I have seen enough for one day."

She'd change her mind. He was sure of that. Sam dressed in a clean shirt and slacks, then gathered up his dirty clothes and ventured barefoot through the set of small rooms and out into the hall. Ruckles waited for him beside an enormous portrait of a lady posing with three ugly dogs.

The butler kept his hands behind his back and rocked on his heels. "Sir?"

"Have you come to lead me out of this maze?"

"Lady Elizabeth would prefer you to confine your explorations to the west wing and has asked that I escort you to your room."

"Don't worry," Sam said, following the old man down the long hallway. "I won't tell her you're the one who showed me where I could take a shower."

"I already explained, sir. I gather you are not injured?"

"No." A few scrapes and bruises were nothing compared to what could have happened. He felt himself shrivel just thinking about it.

"Excellent. Then all is well."

Easy for the butler to say. He hadn't spent all afternoon trying to figure out how to repair a leaky roof, only to end up dangling from the ceiling like an X-rated chandelier.

BETSY WAS BORED. Ruckles had disappeared after bringing another trunk of Longley papers. She was beginning to think the English had had too much time on their hands back in the old days. The fine, spidery lettering of a seventeenth-century correspondent had begun to make her vision blur. She'd read about Oliver Cromwell's brief occupation of Longley. She'd read about art acquired during the fourth earl's trip to "the continent." She'd read about crops, marriages, births and deaths. But she had not read any mention of furniture, and she had not found any interesting journal entries dated in the 1500s.

There was no one to talk to. Sam had dropped by twice before lunch, but hadn't been seen since. Lady Elizabeth had dropped in for a brief chat when she'd returned home from her afternoon jaunt. The lovely young woman had taken all the guests on a drive around the country. Betsy strolled over to the window and admired the blue sky. She would have given a lot to see a cottage Jane Austen had lived in, also, but there would be plenty of time for that once Sam and Elizabeth were married.

She'd been invited to join everyone for tea in the medieval kitchen. If she felt up to it, naturally. There was to be a visit to the jewel closet before dinner, and a local chorus was coming to sing for the guests after dinner. Peggie, in between cleaning chores, had told her there would be chicken pot pie for dinner and three kinds of desserts.

Betsy climbed out of bed and did a number of jumping jacks. She still knew nothing more about the queen's bed, but she knew a great deal more about Ruckles's book. The man was a genius, but he lacked a certain flair for the dramatic that would make his book appeal to readers. She'd read the first two chapters and knew immediately they would need livening up. Anyone who read it would be asleep in less than ten minutes.

Betsy was on her thirteenth sit-up when she heard footsteps, lots of them, coming down the hall. She brightened and got to her feet. If the guests were restless, maybe they could be enticed into her room for some conversation. She opened the door and peeked out. No Sam. No Elizabeth. But a herd of women who looked as if they had had an adventure.

"Hello!" she called, and invited them in. "Are you lost?"

"Peggie is taking us to the library for tea."

Peggie curtsied to Betsy and winked.

"I thought you were having tea in one of the old kitchens." Betsy climbed back in bed and prepared for a nice long chat.

"We did," the tall one said. "Except—"

She and another lady exchanged looks. As if they were going to start laughing and didn't know if they should.

The maid backed out of the room. "Why don't I bring tea in here, and you can all have a little visit?"

"Wonderful," Betsy agreed and turned to her guests. "What happened?" She loved a good story, and after Ruckles's version of history, anything else would be hysterical.

"Lord Longford had a little accident," the older woman explained. "He fell through the kitchen ceiling."

"He did *what?*"

"Fell through the ceiling," one of the women repeated. "Oh, not all the way. His legs were in the kitchen, but the rest of him—"

"Was upstairs," another woman finished. "Since the ceiling in that room is at least two stories high, I'd guess he was on the third floor. I think he was taking a shower. You know how men like to sing in the shower.''

Betsy leaned forward and tossed the covers aside. She was going to see for herself that her Sam wasn't hurt. Hanging from the ceiling? What had possessed him to do such a silly thing? "Where is he now?"

The silver-haired woman touched her arm. "He's fine, Mrs. Martin. I heard Ruckles say so himself."

"I'll believe it when I see it," she murmured, but she replaced the satin cover.

"I think he's probably getting dressed now. We watched from the doorway and heard Lady Elizabeth help him get out of the hole. He sounded fine from what we could hear." The women looked at her and nodded.

"He had been in the shower?"

"That's what we gathered."

"So he was naked when he fell?"

They nodded, displaying assorted expressions of amusement.

"And Lady Elizabeth was with him?"

Again they agreed.

"Wonderful," Betsy sighed, resting on the pillows. "That is absolutely wonderful." She remembered her manners and picked up a pile of letters. "Would you like to hear about my historical research?"

SHE HAD LOST HER MIND, her temper and her guests. The library was empty, with not so much as a short-bread crumb to show that anyone had been there. The fire, providing the only light in the long room, burned cheerfully behind the grate, so Elizabeth poured herself a glass of sherry and sat down in her grandfather's leather chair to contemplate her future.

Futures were shaky things. Like marriages and inheritances and the whims of a very conservative board of trustees. Futures were something to fear or something to plan for. Most importantly, they were tricky. Just when she thought she had it all figured out, wham! Fate had a way of changing the plans. A husband walked out, an inheritance turned out to be filled with legal stipulations, and aging, powerful men debated every shilling spent on renovating a house that would take several lifetimes to repair, and which they would prefer to sell.

Elizabeth took a large swallow of her drink and stretched her legs in front of the fire. The solitude could be called medicinal, along with the drink. Perhaps her guests were lost. Or had also fallen through holes in the floor and were now shrieking ''Help'' from the wine cellar.

She would let them shriek. She had changed into fresh slacks and a clean white blouse, she was going to drink her sherry and assume that everyone was having tea in the dining room. Perhaps Ruckles had misunderstood her directions. Elizabeth leaned her head back in her chair and debated whether or not to start searching. She heard footsteps in the hall and knew exactly who they belonged to. Drat.

"No tea?"

She should have known that he would find her. Since his was the last voice she wanted to hear, she didn't turn to the door to welcome him inside. "There is tea somewhere in the house, but not here."

Sam entered the room and went over to the decanters on the side table. "In that case I'll have scotch."

"Help yourself."

He already had. And then he sat down in the chair beside her and faced the fire. "Aren't you going to ask me how I am?"

"No. I'm sure you're fine. Your kind always is."

"My kind?" He rattled the ice cubes in his glass. "What exactly is my 'kind'? The kind of man who travels with his mother? The kind of man who wears silly clothes and steps on ladies' dresses? The kind of man who falls naked through ceilings, the kind—"

"Oh, do be quiet. You know what I mean."

"Why don't you tell me," he said, his voice turning serious.

"You know. You're a man."

He sighed. "I see. You had a son of a bitch for

an ex-husband, right? He was the one who was supposed to show up here for the weekend."

"Anthony. Yes. He's my cousin. A very distant one, but, as the only male Longford left, he inherited the title when my grandfather died. My father was an only child and died when I was two."

"And you conveniently married Anthony to keep the estate?"

"Not exactly." Though naturally that was what everyone assumed. "The estate went to a trust. My grandfather set it up to avoid some of the costly inheritance taxes. The trustees reluctantly appointed me as the caretaker. I can live here—along with my children and grandchildren—as long as Longley generates a certain amount of income. I'd had a crush on Anthony for years. What I didn't know was why he married *me*."

Sam turned to look at her. "I would think it would be obvious."

She shook her head. "I think he felt sorry for me. My mother died when I was twelve and I was raised in this house by my grandfather. I was *not* a pretty child. And there really isn't a lot of money here. Not what it looks like, anyway. The paintings, the silver, anything of value is held in trust and can't be sold, not even to put on a new roof."

"That's not what—never mind." He put his drink

on the table between them and leaned toward her. "What did Anthony the son of a bitch do?"

"He liked other women. Lots of them. He had an inheritance coming to him when he married, you see. The title, the money and the estate all seemed perfect."

"And what about the wife?"

"The wife was too much in love to understand that her charming husband didn't intend to stay and take care of Longley."

"You can't really blame the man. Longley must be a full-time job."

She smiled ruefully. "I don't blame him for not wanting to save the estate. It was my home not his." *I blame myself because he didn't want me.* She forced a smile on her face. "I'm trying to keep it as it was, but I hope it doesn't fall down around my ears."

He picked up his drink and turned toward the fire again. "It just about fell down around mine today."

"Please tell me you're not suing me. I've heard that Americans sue over everything."

"I'm not suing you, Lizzie. Despite being a man *and* and American, I'm really not a bad guy."

"I behaved badly. I apologize."

"And I provoked you." His soft chuckle was completely disarming.

"You can stay until Monday," she offered. "And I'm sorry I told Ruckles to pack your bags."

"You did? I mean, you are?"

"Yes," Elizabeth admitted, filled with remorse. He'd almost been killed in her house. His mother had fallen ill in her house. She owed them the weekend, at least.

He seemed to think that over. "First thing in the morning I'll see that the hole is boarded over."

She was too tired to protest the offer, especially since she wouldn't be able to find a carpenter until Monday morning. "I would really appreciate that."

"One thing, though."

Her heart sank. What did he want now?

"Ruckles will have to show me the way. I still don't know how to get around this place without getting lost." He held his glass out and touched it to hers. "Truce?"

"Truce," she agreed. He had the most wonderful brown eyes. "It's been a very strange twenty-four hours."

"From now on," Sam promised, "things should quiet down."

"A GHOST?"

"That's what she said. The ghost of Queen Elizabeth herself, right in that bedroom."

"My mother has a very active imagination, Mrs. Canfield. Are you sure—"

"Oh, yes. We heard all about it. Your mother invited us to her room for tea and showed us her research and then told us about the ghost. Ellen and Marje took notes."

"We were passing by her room, after your, um, accident this afternoon," Barbara explained. "We're so glad to see that you weren't hurt."

"Thank you. It was quite a shock."

"For all of us," the lady agreed. "But visiting with your mother was so much fun."

"I apologize for frightening you during your tea. How did you like the old kitchen? There aren't many like that left in England, I hear."

"It was wonderful, but tell me, are there any other rooms in the house that are haunted?"

Sam looked to the other end of the dining room table for help. Lizzie, intent on the conversation between two other women, didn't notice. "Not that I know of."

"Your mother is so much fun. We were supposed to have toured the jewel closet before dinner, but we ran out of time. Lady Elizabeth said we will get to do it tomorrow, after a trip to town."

Phyllis Nolan leaned forward. "You should have told us that your butler was writing a book. I would love to read it when it's done."

Ms. Lee nodded. "I've always wanted to write a book. Someday I will, when I have the time."

"This casserole is delicious," he said. "I must tell the cook how much we enjoyed it."

The lady to his right, the one from New York, spoke up. "My cousin's sister-in-law is an agent in New York. I can ask her if she's interested in English history books. And ghost stories."

"I really don't think there are ghosts here at Longley," Sam said. "What exactly did my mother tell you?"

"That the ghost of Queen Elizabeth visits the blue bedroom, and yesterday Mrs. Martin herself sensed her presence and fainted dead away."

"And this morning, when that nice maid dropped the breakfast tray, she ran into something."

"Something invisible," someone else added.

Sam looked at the four women and picked up the dish of carrots. "Would anyone like more vegetables?"

"Do you grow them here on the estate?"

He had no idea. "Of course," he replied. "The British are very self-sufficient."

Of course they agreed with him.

"Have you ever seen a ghost here?"

Sam shook his head. "No. And I don't think I want to."

"Has anything ever frightened you?"

He looked down the table at Elizabeth's gorgeous face. Hell, yes. There was one thing at Longley that scared him half to death.

7

"NO, MADAM, I am not going to tell you."

"Oh, come on, Ruckles. Sam was naked. Lady E. was there with him. Surely something must have happened." She tossed a dusty journal aside and rose from the chair. "I'm not going to read another historical word unless you talk."

The butler stood stiff and silent for a long moment. "Lady Elizabeth aided your son in his time of need."

"Meaning?"

"I believe she was instrumental in his release from the ceiling."

"I heard he was naked at the time. Is that true?"

Ruckles frowned. "Mr. Martin, I believe, had recently finished bathing and had yet to dress."

Betsy put her hands on her hips. No butler was going to gyp her out of a good story. And there had to be a good story or Ruckles wouldn't have that prune face on. "Go on. What else?"

He sighed. "When I entered the room, Lady Elizabeth was um, covering your son's, ah, nudity."

"With what?" Now this was getting intriguing.

Ruckles coughed. "With herself, madam."

"She was on *top* of him?"

"Partially, I believe. I would assume they had fallen backward after releasing his er, thigh from its predicament."

"I see." She wanted to jump up and down with joy, but she restrained herself and walked over to the portrait of the queen instead. "I knew it," she said.

"Knew what?"

"That they were perfect for each other. Your lady needs a man and my Sammy needs to settle down."

"You may have an excellent point, madam. Your son has repaired the section of an overhang that created a puddle in one of the paths to the kitchen. And I believe this morning he is going to attempt to repair the hole in the ceiling."

"See? Perfect for Longley." And Longley was the perfect place for grandchildren. So many places to play hide-and-seek. So many wonderful gardens. Betsy pictured tea parties and little girls in white pinafores.

"Exceedingly more helpful than the previous husband," Ruckles admitted. "Lord Anthony was a bit on the useless side. And he demanded to be waited on past ten o'clock."

"Sam is an early to bed, early to rise man."

"I've noticed." Ruckles nodded his approval.

"And once he learns his way around the estate, he won't need me at all."

"More time to write," she assured him. "We may need to speed things up a little."

"Keep me informed, if you would. Right at this moment I," proclaimed the butler, "need to finish chapter three. If you will excuse me?"

Betsy didn't take her gaze from the portrait. "Maybe I'm wrong. Maybe the room isn't haunted. Maybe it's the portrait itself."

Ruckles stood beside her and considered the question as he stared at the red-haired queen. "That's a possibility, I suppose, if you are determined to pursue this ghost business. I should be able to research the history of the painting. All of the art at Longley was catalogued in my father's time. Lady E. would know."

She sighed. "I've found nothing to show that the queen ever slept here in Longley, but I'm convinced this room is haunted. I can feel it. Surely some of the Longley ancestors felt it, too."

"There are trunks of records that have never been examined, at least not in this century. Tomorrow I will attempt to extract them from the nurseries, but for now I will see if I can finish my chapter on the second earl and his diplomatic efforts in Europe."

Not exactly something for the *New York Times* bestseller list. Betsy turned and gestured toward the stacks of correspondence and journals. "I've made notes, but most of these deal with the everyday life of the family. They were a very prolific group, weren't they?"

"I have not studied that aspect of the family."

"Take my word for it." She collapsed into the chair again. "This is a beautiful room. I can see why a queen would haunt it."

"I wish she would haunt the music room and put an end to the evening," the old man said. "I am extremely weary of English ballads, although the guests seem to be enjoying the performance."

"Is that what they're singing? I can barely hear, even when I went out into the hall."

"They are madrigal singers, madam. A local group. And they are singing English ballads. Quite tiresome," he grumbled. "I prefer Andrew Lloyd Webber."

"Me, too." Betsy yawned and stretched her arms over her head. "Don't forget to bring me those trunks in the morning, Ruckles. I'm in the mood to find a ghost. *And* a daughter-in-law."

"Very good, madam." He bowed and left the room, leaving Betsy staring at the painting and willing the queen to give her some help.

Time was running out.

"MRS. MARTIN, you really shouldn't have told my guests that Longley is haunted." Elizabeth hoped her tone was patient yet firm. She'd brought Sam's mother's breakfast tray and hoped she could convince her to stick to the truth. The silver-haired little lady in the wide bed didn't look like someone who could cause so much trouble, but Elizabeth was learning differently.

"Oh, dear." Mrs. Martin's forehead wrinkled. "Have I done something wrong? I thought I would entertain the ladies. They were wandering the halls and wondering what to do with themselves."

"They were?"

"Why, yes, dear. They were quite upset over Sam's fall, you know, and so was I. So I ordered tea sent up to my room and diverted them with stories of Longley." She patted the pile of papers on the bed. "I've been studying, you know."

Elizabeth pulled the small chair over to the bed and sat down. She'd been awake since five, preparing breakfast and arranging the day's events. She'd slept for only three hours. Lying awake thinking about a handsome, brown-eyed American had given her a headache, and yet Sam's mother had a way of holding one's attention. "Studying what exactly?"

"Didn't you know? I'm helping Mr. Ruckles with his research. We're trying to find any mention of the queen's visit to Longley."

"I wasn't aware she visited here. This was the

earl's second country home and not typically available for entertaining.''

Betsy sighed. "I know, but ever since I walked into this room, I've felt her presence. I just know she's here.''

Elizabeth prayed for another dose of patience. "But you can't tell people that the queen is haunting the house.''

"Why not? It's true.''

"I've never seen a ghost, and I've lived here all my life.''

"Maybe you're just used to her and don't even notice.''

"Mrs. Martin, I think if I saw a ghost I would notice. And remember.''

"So would I,'' Sam said, stepping into the room. "Mother, you have to stop telling stories. Good morning, Lizzie. I missed you at breakfast.''

"I was in the kitchen.''

"I know. I looked. I must have just missed you.''

"Good morning.'' He'd looked for her. He missed her at breakfast. Those were nice things to say.

"Good morning, Sam,'' Betsy said, smiling as he walked around to the other side of the bed and kissed her cheek. "You're up bright and early.''

He looked at his watch. "It's after eight already. I've been up for hours.'' Sam touched the pile of envelopes. "I see you're still reading. Were there ghost stories in there, too?"

"A few," she said, making Elizabeth groan. "They're rather bloody, nothing at all what I'm looking for."

"Oh, please don't encourage her." Elizabeth looked across the bed at him and wondered about the dark circles under his eyes. Had he slept as badly as she?

"Encourage her about what?"

"Anything about the queen."

Sam looked at Elizabeth before turning back to his mother. She swore he was almost sympathetic. "The ladies at dinner last night were telling me about their visit with you."

"We had a *lovely* time."

"I heard. They were thrilled with the stories." He sat on the edge of the bed, and Betsy moved her legs to make room for him.

"They were thrilled about it?" Elizabeth didn't believe that for a minute.

"Yes," Sam said. "Didn't they tell you?"

"Well, yes, but I thought they were a bit frightened."

Betsy patted Elizabeth's hand. "People love to be frightened, my dear. Believe me, I know what I'm talking about. Ghosts might be good for your tourist business."

"That's not why I want people to come to Longley, Mrs. Martin." She glanced over to Sam for help. "We have a lot of history here, a heritage. I'd like people to appreciate Longley as a beautiful building and a family home that has survived more than five hundred years."

Betsy waved her hand, dismissing that notion. "That's all well and good, but having a ghost is better."

"I don't think Lady Elizabeth wants her home to be turned into a carnival." Sam's voice was gentle.

"No one could mistake Longley for a carnival, Sammy. It's much too beautiful."

Elizabeth didn't know how to argue with that statement, so she decided that history would be a safer topic than ghosts. "Have you discovered anything unusual about my ancestors? I know Ruckles is compiling information for his book, but he is only at the beginning."

"Nothing earthshaking. The letters are a bit mixed up, and so are the journals. I never know what I'm going to find. There do seem to be a lot of births and deaths recorded, and the Longfords were involved in politics. Very diplomatic people."

Sam's eyebrows rose. "Diplomatic?"

Elizabeth met his gaze. "I take after my mother."

"No kidding."

Betsy patted Elizabeth's hand. "There's nothing

wrong with a woman who speaks her mind. The women Sam usually dates simper and flutter and hang on his every word."

"Simper? I don't think they *simper*. Just because they find me fascinating doesn't mean—"

"Oh, really, Sam. It's nauseating. Where do you find these women?"

He got up from the bed and went to the door. "I refuse to discuss my personal life with a woman who's been making up ghost stories."

"Which has livened things up around here." She gave Elizabeth an arch look. "No offense, dear, but this place needs a little more excitement."

More excitement? She glanced toward Sam, who looked as incredulous as she felt. "Mrs. Martin, in the last thirty-six hours I've acquired ten very important guests, a hole in my ceiling, a husband, a mother-in-law and an artificial ghost. It has been lovely meeting you, but I'm quite sure I don't need any further excitement."

"Look on the bright side," Sam said, patting her on the shoulder. "Did you notice I fixed your puddle?"

"You did?" She was as amazed by that as she was by the warmth of his hand.

"You need a new roof, but I fixed that overhang. Temporarily."

She needed a lot of things, including a roof. But

most of all she needed a man like Sam. Too bad he was only temporary, too. "Thank you, but you didn't have to do that."

He shrugged and moved toward the door. "I enjoyed it. Are you joining me for breakfast?"

"Yes, in a few minutes."

"Good idea," Betsy said. "You should spend more time together and act like a happily married couple. You want your guests to think we're one big happy family, don't you?"

Sam blew her—or his mother?—a kiss. With that he was gone, his footsteps echoing down the corridor.

"He's very handy to have around," Mrs. Martin said, in her not-so-subtle way. "He'd make some lucky woman a nice husband."

"I'm sure he would," Elizabeth said, standing up and placing the chair back against the wall. "If one were in the market for one."

"And you're not, dear? Don't tell me that a lovely young lady like you isn't interested in marriage."

Elizabeth paused by the door and looked into the older woman's kind blue eyes. "I was married once, Mrs. Martin. Not even someone like your son could tempt me to do it again."

The woman didn't look as if she believed a word of it. "Be that as it may, I'm going to keep on with my research for Ruckles. He's bringing in more trunks and boxes today, so with any luck we'll find the century we're looking for. Some of the ladies offered to help, so the work should go faster.''

"The ladies? My ladies?''

"They said they couldn't wait.'' Mrs. Martin bit her lower lip. "You don't mind, do you?''

"Well—''

"It's such a rainy morning. A little reading will keep us all busy.''

"As long as they're happy,'' Elizabeth conceded. "I was going to take them to the Old Stokes Church and then on to Stonehenge.''

"That does sound like more fun than reading journals, but maybe some of the guests won't want to look at those old stones when it's raining as hard as this.''

"You could be right.'' She'd had other ideas for a rainy weekend, but none of them compared with Mrs. Martin's search for the supernatural.

Mrs. Martin beamed. "We'll let you know if we find anything interesting.''

She prayed they wouldn't. "And no more ghost stories?''

"Don't spoil our fun,'' Sam's mother cautioned. "The facts are the facts, after all.''

"Just don't get carried away,'' Elizabeth warned. "I don't want anyone having nightmares.''

"Strictly history, I promise. Ruckles is going to

look for some kind of record of the paintings. And he's going to bring us more trunks full of papers, too.''

''I think the art was catalogued before my grandfather died. There would be a record of that in one of the drawing rooms. I'd be happy to get it for you, but I don't know what help it will be.''

''You never know what will turn up,'' Mrs. Martin chirped, picking up her teacup. ''Every little bit helps.''

''I'll try to find those papers after breakfast,'' Elizabeth promised. She slipped out of the room and into the hall. At first the house seemed surprisingly silent, but as she approached the staircase she heard someone whistling ''Yankee Doodle Dandy.''

For all the aggravation Sam had brought with him to Longley, the man certainly knew how to make her smile. His mother was a little eccentric, but terribly sweet. And Sam had fixed the puddle for her.

She refused to fall in love with him.

She absolutely refused, she repeated, chanting the words under her breath as she went downstairs to join him for breakfast.

''WHAT THE HELL is all this stuff?'' Sam took three steps into what looked as if it had once been a living room. All of a sudden his feet felt as big as snowshoes as he stepped past a row of blue-and-white vases.

"Ancient Chinese porcelain. Be careful. I've been trying to catalogue it, and there are pieces scattered everywhere." Elizabeth pointed to an enormous table whose surface was covered in porcelain bowls, pots, dishes, figurines, jars and bottles. "It's my project for the winter. We put it in one of the drawing rooms so it would be easy to access."

"I've never seen anything like this before."

"Not too many people have," Elizabeth said, touching a bowl with reverent fingers. "Last summer I discovered that the fifth earl's collection was most likely very valuable. It's rare to have this many pieces of seventeenth-century porcelain in one place."

"What are you going to do with it?"

"As soon as I can get it catalogued, I'll call in an expert and we'll arrange a show. I'm hoping the exhibit will draw more visitors to Longley next year."

Sam pictured hordes of tourists dressed in blue and white.

"We need something to make us stand out from the other houses," Elizabeth said. "This might attract some attention next spring."

"More than the ghost of Queen Elizabeth?"

"Don't joke about such a thing." Elizabeth shuddered. "I'd be the laughingstock of the neighborhood."

"Why?"

"There is no reason to believe that Queen Elizabeth ever visited here. She was supposed to, according to the family stories, but her visit was canceled when one of the earl's daughters came down with a fever. Smallpox, I imagine. The queen slept elsewhere, which would have been a great disappointment to the family." She began making her way through the room, peering behind chairs and sofas.

"Does Ruckles know this?"

"He's heard the stories, but of course he'd like to prove that the queen actually returned at a later date. He is certain that such a discovery would elevate Longley's position if we could say the queen slept here."

"In the blue bedroom," Sam added.

She moved to the other side of the table and examined a stack of magazines. "Possibly. The furniture was moved around quite a bit in my grandmother's day when she modernized parts of the house."

"Can I help you look?"

"Sure. They're brown leather, three volumes, with—"

Crash. Something heavy above them fell, shaking the library's plaster ceiling. A decorative chunk of plaster the size of a pie plate shook loose from the ceiling and crashed to the floor, narrowly missing the collection of porcelain spread across the wide table, but shattering something on the carpet when it landed.

Elizabeth put her hands to her face and covered her eyes, but Sam grabbed her and pushed her under the table.

"How much do you think was broken?" she asked, after a long minute of silence. Sam stuck his head out and saw that nothing else was dangling from the ceiling.

"I can't tell from here. This house is going to kill someone. What on earth is above us?"

"Storage rooms. Something must have fallen, but I can't imagine what."

"Unless the whole house is crashing down around us."

She took a deep breath. "At least we weren't injured," she reminded herself, crawling from under the table to inspect the damage. Sam followed her, but he kept a careful eye on the ceiling.

Miraculously the pieces on the table weren't broken. The one casualty was an ugly vase that Sam privately thought had been put out of its misery. Everything else was intact, but Elizabeth hurried back to the table.

"Come," she said. "We have to put these where they will be safe."

"And that is?"

She stopped. "I haven't the faintest idea." She looked at Sam with that helpless expression that made him want to take her in his arms and kiss her until she forgot about pottery, broken or otherwise. "Do you?"

He thought. Quickly. "Under the table."

"I think we're safe now, Sam, but—"

"We put all this sh—stuff under the table. That way if anything else falls, it's protected." He picked up a bowl in each hand. "You get under there and I'll hand them to you."

"Good idea." She hesitated. "I wonder if I should see what happened upstairs first, in case anyone needs help."

He handed her a couple of figurines. "The maids are up there, aren't they?"

"Yes," she said, disappearing under the table for a second.

"If anything's wrong, you'll be the first person they come to find."

"I suppose you're right." She glanced toward the ceiling again, but continued to place porcelain in neat rows under the table until all of the pieces were safe. "I can't imagine what would have happened if we'd lost it all," she murmured.

"You are a very lucky woman," he said, scooping a porcelain bird into his hand and placing it in hers.

"Last piece, safe and sound." Sam bent down and kissed her. Only once. Only for a moment, he promised himself.

Until she kissed him back.

"DID YOU FIND HER?"

Pattie nodded and looked from Ruckles to Betsy and back again. "I did."

"And did you have to tell her what happened?"

"No."

"Good," Betsy whispered. She didn't want the ladies in the bedroom to overhear. They'd been having such a fun time this morning. "That means no harm's been done."

Ruckles's worried expression eased. "Then it won't be necessary to inform Lady Elizabeth of the minor...incident this morning." He turned to Betsy and bowed. "I will check to see if I'm needed downstairs, and then I will return with another trunk."

"For heaven's sake, be careful." If Elizabeth found out that Ruckles was knocking over rolls of carpet in order to dig up old documents, she might put an end to the research once and for all.

Pattie blocked his way to the stairs. "Mr. Ruckles, I don't think you want to disturb Lady E. right now, if you know what I mean."

Betsy leaned closer. "Really?"

The two women exchanged looks. "Yes, Mrs. Martin. Really."

"Lovely."

The butler frowned. "What on earth are you saying?"

Pattie smiled. "Lady E. and her husband are having a private moment in the third drawing room."

"Where the porcelain is stored?"

"Ruckles, you've turned very pale." Betsy took his arm and led him toward a velvet bench. "Sit down and put your head between your knees."

To her amazement he did exactly that. Betsy sat beside him and patted him between his bony shoulder blades. She looked up at Pattie, who looked as if she wanted to be anywhere else. "What kind of a 'private moment' are we talking about?"

Ruckles moaned. "Was anything broken?"

"I couldn't tell."

Betsy frowned. "Is that your answer to my question or Ruckles's?"

"Both, Mrs. Martin. I couldn't tell. Mr. Sam and Lady E. were on the floor kissing, by that big table where the little china things used to be." She rolled her eyes at Betsy. "I hated dusting those little buggers."

Ruckles lifted his head. "*Used* to be? What do you mean, *used to be?*"

"I didn't see them just now. The table was clean as a whistle."

Betsy didn't want to talk about china. "Tell me what was going on, on that floor."

The maid laughed. "I will not! Not even for you, Mrs. Martin."

"Thank the Lord," the butler muttered. "I will not be forced to endure another lecture regarding 'sexual tension' or some such nonsense."

"Don't disturb them," Betsy ordered. "We have less than forty-eight hours to make this work. Lady E. is going to be so happy with Sam."

"Lady Elizabeth is not going to be happy about the porcelain. The storeroom that held the carpet is directly above that particular drawing room. She would have heard the noise. I can only pray that none of the priceless collection was damaged." His head went between his knees again as he gasped for air.

Betsy patted his back again. "Ruckles, hasn't anyone ever told you that sex was more fun than old china?"

8

"THIS IS INSANE."

"You're right." Sam lifted his mouth from the base of Lizzie's neck. She smelled of roses. "We should be in bed."

"We should not." She put her hands on each side of his face and drew him to her for one more kiss. "We should be vertical, with our clothes buttoned neatly."

"No. We should be completely naked, with the doors locked."

"Not a good idea."

He thought it was. He liked his hand where it was, sliding over one very warm, very soft breast. He propped his head up with his other hand. "We should unbutton everything we're wearing and make love to each other right here on this old carpet."

"This 'old carpet' is an eighteenth-century Aubusson and besides, I have to find out what made that horrible noise."

"Maybe it was the ghost of Queen Elizabeth."

"Oh, don't even joke about such a thing."

He smiled. "I'll clean up the broken vase and destroy the evidence."

"Save the pieces, okay? I may be able to have it reglued."

He looked across the room at the mess of broken china. "You must be joking."

She shrugged. "The Longfords never throw anything away. That's why I have three hundred rooms full of stuff." Elizabeth slid away from his touch and began to button her blouse. She ran her fingers through her hair. "I have to make lunch."

"Let the cook do it," he murmured, envisioning spending the afternoon locked in the drawing room with a passionate Englishwoman. He would enjoy unbuttoning that blouse again.

"Oh, Sam. There isn't any cook."

He lifted his head and looked into those blue eyes. "You're the cook, too?"

"Fooled you, did I?"

"Sweetheart, do you ever sleep?"

"Not much," she admitted. "You can't believe how expensive this house is to run."

"And you can't do it all by yourself. And having Ruckles doesn't count."

"I love this place," she said, giving him that level look he had grown used to. "This is my home, my heritage. Haven't you ever loved something so much that you were willing to do almost anything to keep it?"

Sam sat up and thought about it while Elizabeth tucked her blouse into her slacks. "I don't think so. At least not since I was a kid."

Not until now, he wanted to say. But he'd only met her two days ago. No one fell in love in two days. Especially not Sam Martin, a man who wasn't thinking about getting married.

"Then I don't suppose you could understand," Elizabeth said, but she smiled and waved as she left the room and shut the door quietly behind her.

Oh, he understood, all right. He understood that if he fell in love with Lizzie he would be asking for trouble. She wouldn't leave Longley, and he couldn't live in this mausoleum.

Not for all the crumpets in London.

"RUCKLES!" Elizabeth hurried down the hall, past the state rooms and toward the blue bedroom. Her butler sat on a bench in one of the alcoves, his head in his hands. "Are you feeling all right?"

The butler stood, straightened his jacket and squared his shoulders. "Yes, m'lady, of course."

Elizabeth worried over the pallor of his skin. "Has something happened?"

"Happened?" he repeated. "Happened?"

"I heard a terrible noise from the old bedroom

where we've stored quite a few things. You must have heard it, too.''

"Yes, m'lady. Actually, I entered the room myself. A large roll of carpet tipped over and crashed to the floor. There was no damage.'' He took a deep breath. "Was there?''

"No one was hurt?''

"Absolutely not, m'lady.''

"I wonder what could have happened.''

The butler shook his head. "I'm sure I don't know.''

"Where is everyone this morning? I talked to several ladies at breakfast, but wasn't able to see everyone.''

"Several of the guests have been quite content to visit with Mrs. Martin. They are helping sort letters and appear to enjoy chatting it up.''

"And the others?''

"Are scattered throughout the house. Some are in the library reading, Ms. Carmichael and Ms. Lee preferred to sleep late and have their breakfasts brought to them, Ms. Nolan is making phone calls to her office, and Ms. Lizotte is walking laps in the long gallery.''

"I thought I would show them the jewel closet and after lunch we'd venture outside for a jaunt to Stonehenge and a little tour of Bath. I'd like to stick to the schedule as much as possible.''

"Yes, m'lady. I will inform them of the plan. What time will lunch be served?"

"The usual time. One o'clock."

"Very good."

Elizabeth hesitated. "Perhaps I should examine the storeroom and make certain there is nothing wrong. I can't have pieces of plaster falling on the heads of my guests."

"Plaster, m'lady?"

"Yes. One of the decorative roundels was loosened by the vibration. I almost lost the whole lot of porcelain, and Longley almost lost its spring exhibit."

Ruckles turned pale again, so Elizabeth patted him on the arm. "Don't worry. We only lost a vase, and not one of the older ones at that."

"A relief," he agreed. "I have examined the storeroom, m'lady. I am certain there will be no more problems."

"Then I will pop in on my guests and Mrs. Martin, then make us a nice lunch. Maybe you should go downstairs and have a cup of tea. You're still looking a bit peaked."

"Thank you, m'lady. I believe I will, not being accustomed to this much excitement."

Elizabeth recalled her time in the drawing room with Sam and knew precisely how the butler felt.

No PUDDLE. Gone, despite the rain and the dampness in the hallway, the wet spot no longer covered part of the stone path to the kitchen. Elizabeth wondered how Sam had managed to fix it.

He was good at a lot of things. He could whistle. He could sing. He said things that made her laugh. He would be a wonderful lover, not that she had many to compare that to. Anthony had been her one and only lover, and he'd made it clear that she could not and would not compete with the other women he met.

And Anthony, member of the jet set and host of a weekly chat show on the television, met a lot of women.

Sam. How many women had Sam made love to? He had a way of kissing that made her feel as if her clothes were melting from the heat of her skin.

Elizabeth opened the kitchen door and tried to stop thinking about sex. Peggie was busy peeling carrots, but she looked up and greeted her. Soup was bubbling on the stove.

"I thought I'd better get it started," the maid explained. "You left it out to thaw for lunch, right?"

"Absolutely." Thawing. That was how she felt, all mushy and warm. Anthony had left two years ago. A long time to be without someone to love.

"M'lady?"

Elizabeth looked over to Peggie. "Yes?"

"I asked if you wanted me to heat the bread or just slice it and put it in baskets. I made chicken salad and tuna salad and sliced up some peaches."

"Slicing it is fine, whatever you like. You didn't have to do all of that by yourself."

"I like to cook," the maid said. "Pattie would rather clean and fuss with the furniture, but I like the kitchen." She wiped her hands on her apron. "The desserts were delivered a bit ago. The cheesecake is in the fridge and the little cookies are still wrapped tight."

"Lovely. Thank you."

"You're welcome, m'lady. You don't have to be in here, you know. Why don't you go find Mr. Sam and take a nice walk?"

"It's raining."

The maid shrugged. "Only a little. Has he seen the pond? Men like ponds. My Albert has taken some nice-sized trout from that pond, and he says there's lots more to be had for the right fisherman."

"I don't know if Mr. Sam fishes." There was a lot she didn't know about "Mr. Sam." Like what he did for a living. And what his hobbies were. And if he knew she was falling in love with him.

"Ask him."

As if it would be that simple. "He fixed the puddle."

Pattie winked. "A handy man to have around, that's for sure. Maybe he'd like a job."

"I'm sure he will be on his way to London on Monday. Mrs. Martin seems to be feeling better. And he doesn't look like the kind of man who needs work."

"You never know until you ask. His mother's a dear one," the maid said. "She'd probably tell you."

"Pattie, how did you know you were in love with Johnny?"

"From the first minute I saw him. He sat beside me on the train to London, and by the time we arrived at Paddington Station, I was in love."

"How did you know?"

"It was his hands, m'lady. I looked at those hands and those blue eyes and I said to myself, "Pattie, my girl, don't let this one get away.""

"What did you do?"

"I smiled and gave him my phone number. And when he called me, I asked him to dinner and made him a nice roast beef with all the trimmings. He met my ma and my da and my cats, and he kissed me good-night."

"And?" Elizabeth prompted, fascinated by the simplicity of the romance.

"Two weeks later he took me to his cottage and asked me to marry him."

"It was that easy?"

"Love is easy, m'lady. Or it should be, if it's right." She picked up a knife and began slicing a crusty loaf of bread.

If it's right. If it's love. But did anyone fall in love in two days except characters in books? Sam wouldn't want her. He would be taking on Longley, too. She'd learned the hard way that no one in their right mind would willingly take on this estate. He would be trapped inside a lovely old monster that ate money twenty-four hours a day. He would fall through floors and fix puddles and avoid tourists. He would be as miserable as Anthony had been.

And this time it would break her heart.

"TONIGHT'S THE NIGHT," Betsy whispered. "I'm sure you can come up with something."

Ruckles drew himself to his full height and looked down his long nose. "Madam, I cannot possibly move Mr. Sam's luggage into Lady E.'s room without her permission."

"Of course you can. Just say that one of the guests complained that her companion snored. The two young ladies from Connecticut are sharing a room, aren't they?"

"Yes, but—"

"Or you can say that the guests are getting suspicious, that someone saw Sam going into a different room down the hall from Elizabeth's."

"She would never believe that one."

"You have to try, Ruckles. We have one night left, then it's back to America for me and back to butlering for you," she reminded him. "No more help with your research, no more editorial advice, no more brainstorming plot ideas. You'll be back to opening doors and fixing holes and following Lady Elizabeth around the house." She knew she was making progress by the way his knuckles turned white as he clasped his hands in front of him. "You can turn a bunch of those duties over to Sam once they're married. And who knows? Maybe you can just retire and write."

"Retire?"

"It's not half-bad. Trust me, I just did it and I've never had so much fun in my life."

"Fun?" He spoke the word as if he'd never heard it before.

"Fun," she repeated. "The three-letter *F* word that means you get to do anything you want to do, anytime you want to do it. Look at me, for example. Don't I look like I'm having fun?"

"You, madam, begging your pardon, look as if you are always on the verge of trouble."

"Trouble is fun, too," she said, herding him toward the door. "Now, go pack Sam's things, but don't move them into her room until dinner. I'll keep them busy after dinner. By the time they realize they're sleeping together, it will be too late to do anything about it.''

"I could lose my job.''

"No one's losing anything," she promised, giving him a push. "Now *go,* while Sam's busy fixing the floor. It's time to take the bull by the horns.''

"DO YOU HAVE anything planned for us tonight, Lady Elizabeth?''

Sam looked up from slicing an exceptionally tender piece of roast beef. He would have liked to ask that question himself, in private. Lizzie was all dressed up tonight in a pale blue dress and a delicate diamond necklace he assumed was genuine. No one would guess that the elegant woman had been cooking their dinner an hour ago.

Elizabeth smiled. "I thought I would let you have a quiet evening tonight, since we're eating dinner so late, and we spent all afternoon walking up and down the streets of Bath, but if anyone would like to go out, we could visit a pub in the village.''

The idea was met with silence.

"In that case," she said, "I'd like to open some special champagne and toast our guests. It has been a lovely weekend, and I hope you have enjoyed yourselves.''

Everyone said they had, and Elizabeth promised a celebration with dessert. Betsy, who had felt well enough to come downstairs and join the party for dinner, offered to discuss the history of the house with those ladies who had spent the morning with her. "I've found some things that might be of interest," she said.

Sam had to ask. "Like what, Mother? Another ghost? Another haunted room?"

Elizabeth gave him a look that said *don't encourage her.*

"No, the painting is not what's haunted. We discovered, from the records that Elizabeth found for us, that that painting wasn't done until the early 1700s and has no connection to the queen except that the artist painted her."

Some of the ladies groaned.

"So the room isn't haunted," Elizabeth declared. "Would anyone like another serving of carrots?"

"I would, darling," Sam said. Pattie took the bowl from the sideboard and placed it before him on the table. "The vegetables are excellent tonight."

"The room still has *that feeling*," Betsy said, "but we don't know why. If she never visited Longley, why would she be attached to this place?"

"Do ghosts lose their sense of direction?"

Sam started to laugh, then realized the woman beside him was serious. "I don't think so, but I'm not a ghost expert."

"Neither am I," his mother said, sighing. "But there is something about that room." She looked over to Elizabeth. "Are you sure the queen never slept in that bed?"

"As far as I know, Mrs. Martin, the queen's visit was canceled, even though that particular room had been prepared for her."

Betsy nodded. "I found a description of the preparations. The bed was redecorated with crimson silk, with four plumes above the canopy. I'll bet it was quite impressive."

"A haunted bed," one of the guests sighed. "How romantic."

Elizabeth shook her head. "The bed in the blue room isn't the original sixteenth-century bed that was prepared for the queen."

"Where did it go?"

"In my room. It's been there for years, and I've never seen a ghost. I'm sorry, Mrs. Martin."

"Oh, shoot," Betsy muttered. "There goes my last theory."

Sam had endured dessert in the drawing room, he'd listened to the ladies discuss British history, he'd even admired the collection of antique gowns Elizabeth had brought downstairs to show her guests. There was to be a Longley Costume Collection in two years, after the dresses had been repaired and cleaned. Lady Elizabeth had a lot of plans. Her guests were impressed. Her "country weekend" appeared to be a success. Tomorrow everyone would leave, and so would he.

The thought gave him no pleasure. He'd spent the day fixing the floor, he'd taken a long walk around the grounds, he'd seen enormous distant outbuildings going to waste. It seemed to Sam that there were plenty of ways for Longley to make money, but Elizabeth hadn't looked beyond the house.

Once released from his duties as a genial and charming host, Sam excused himself and sat in the library nursing a scotch and pondering his future.

There wasn't much to ponder. He was at a crossroads, and he damn well knew it. He had to admit it—if only to himself—that he was enjoying himself here. He was tired of work. He was ready for something new. He might even have fallen in love. He might even be as crazy as his mother. When he emptied the glass, he left the library and walked down the long west corridor to his room. He'd grown accustomed to green satin and yellow-striped wallpaper, but when he approached the door he found it locked. He rattled the knob and knocked on the thick wood, but nothing happened.

''Sir?'' Ruckles appeared beside him. ''May I help?''

''I've been locked out of my room.''

''No, sir, weren't you told?'' Ruckles frowned and wrung his hands. ''Your room was given to one of the guests. She is traveling with her cousin, you see, and the cousin snores. She requested her own room, and since yours was the only one available—"

"You gave it to her," Sam finished for him. "What do you mean, there are no other rooms available?"

"We're quite full, sir. They are only a certain number of rooms that are fit for company."

Sam was too tired to argue. "Well, show me where I'm to sleep."

He nodded. "I took the liberty of packing your things and moving you to the other end of the hall into Lady E.'s rooms."

"And Lady E. approved of this move?" Sam remembered kissing her under the table this morning. Maybe the lady had changed her mind.

Ruckles cleared his throat. With disapproval, Sam assumed. "Follow me," the man said, walking down the dark hall with stiff strides. He went to the end and opened the door to reveal a pale blue sitting room. Two love seats were placed by the fireplace. A small fire lit the room along with a lamp on a delicate cherry desk. Sam's duffel bags sat beside a chair in the corner, beneath a long lace-curtained window.

"I believe you will be comfortable here," the butler said. He motioned toward a bottle of wine and two glasses positioned on a side table.

"Thanks, Ruckles. Where am I supposed to sleep?" He looked around for the bed, but a set of double doors on the opposite side of the room was closed. He wondered if Lizzie intended for him to sleep on one of those little couches.

"You will find extra bedding in the dressing room." Ruckles went to the door and hesitated before opening it. "And may I say, sir, I hope you enjoyed your stay at Longley. Your help fixing the bathroom floor was greatly appreciated."

"No problem."

The man nodded and left the room, closing the door behind him with a quiet click and leaving Sam alone to explore. The wide doors led to a bedroom. An enormous four-poster bed was covered with a dark blue comforter and white lace pillows. The carpet and walls were ivory colored; small paintings of flowers hung between the windows. Off to one side was a dressing room, which led to a bathroom.

And a woman splashing in the bathtub.

"Lizzie?" He spoke through the inch-wide opening in the door.

The splashing stopped. "Sam?"

"I just thought you should know that I'm here."

A few moments passed. "What are you doing?"

"I'm going to fix myself a drink and figure out where I'm supposed to sleep."

"But why—never mind. I'll be out in a minute."

He could wait. He loosened the top buttons of his shirt and returned to the living room and poured a small amount of wine into one of the glasses. He didn't have long to wait. The lady, wrapped in a floor-length white velvet robe, appeared barefoot in the doorway. She wasn't smiling.

"What are you doing here?"

"Ruckles brought me. He had to give my room to one of the guests and said that you told him to install me in here."

Her lovely mouth opened and closed. "This is a joke, isn't it?"

He shook his head and pointed to the pile of luggage. "Nope. Would you like a glass of wine? Ruckles provided that, too."

She sat on the couch and accepted the glass he put in her hand. "Your mother has something to do with this."

"Probably." He clicked his glass against hers. "What shall we drink to?"

"I can't do this," she moaned, turning that blue-eyed gaze on him.

"Can't do what?"

"Make love to you and then wave goodbye like nothing happened."

He smiled and sat down on the opposite couch, his knees almost touching hers, and leaned forward. "Could we take this one step at a time?"

"Not that it's not tempting, you see, because you're wonderful when you're not being aggravating, but I've finally grown accustomed to being alone and—"

"Elizabeth," he said, halting the flow of words. "Drink your wine and shut up for a minute."

"Okay." She took a sip of the wine. "Merlot. My favorite. Ruckles thought of everything."

"He's being guided by my mother. She's been matchmaking for years."

"Unsuccessfully."

"Yeah. Until now." He took a long swallow of wine. "Lizzie, you're not wearing anything underneath that robe, are you?"

Her cheeks turned pink and she shook her head. "No."

"Then get your cute little rear in your bedroom and shut those damn doors. If not, we're going to be on the floor together in about three minutes."

"Really?"

"Really."

She leaned closer and kissed him. "I've never made love on a floor before."

"Is that a yes?"

Elizabeth tossed her wineglass into the fireplace. "I've always wanted to do that," she said, then turned to Sam. "Are you going to act like a husband or not?"

She didn't have to ask him twice.

9

PERHAPS THE SECRET to spectacular lovemaking was not to use a bed, Elizabeth mused, waking to find her head cushioned by Sam's shoulder. The fire had long since turned to ashes, though she thought she remembered Sam tossing another log into the fireplace sometime during the night.

They were both snuggled on the carpet, covered enough by her robe to feel warm. Apparently a man's naked body radiated quite a bit of heat. He was asleep, his chest rising and falling in a rhythmic motion.

Elizabeth turned toward him and ran her fingertips lightly along his chest. She didn't want to wake him, but she couldn't resist touching him one last time. Morning had arrived, and she would have to bathe and dress and start cooking breakfast.

And Sam would be leaving.

"Hey," Sam murmured, opening his eyes and smiling at her. He looked as handsome as ever with a day-old beard and his hair rumpled.

"Good morning." She told herself she shouldn't

be shy. She had made love to this man twice last night. He had touched her in ways she'd never been touched; he'd fit himself inside of her and made love to her until they were both satisfied and breathless.

"I guess we never made it to the bed," he said.

"No."

Which was good. Her bed would have no memories of him. She could easily find another rug for her room, if she wanted to forget that she had fallen in love. Which maybe she didn't, at least not right away. She wanted to savor the feeling, before he left. Before it was over.

"What are you thinking?"

"Why?"

"You're smiling." Sam urged her closer and she went willingly, until she was on top of him and the robe was tangled around their feet.

"I was thinking of breakfast."

"Liar," he said, lifting her hips and fitting himself inside of her. Elizabeth leaned forward, her hair brushing his cheeks, and kissed him while he filled her.

"Sausage and eggs," Elizabeth recited. "Scones with clotted cream and strawberry—oh, that feels good."

"It's a 'husband' thing," he said, and proceeded to demonstrate until they collapsed side by side between the couches.

"Maybe the guests could made their own breakfast," Elizabeth said when she caught her breath.

"Tell you what," Sam said, turning to face her. He swept a strand of hair from her face. "If my mother refuses to get out of the blue bed, and I refuse to get out of your bed, you'll have to let us stay."

Her heart lifted. "I thought you couldn't wait to leave."

"I can wait," he said. "I think we have some talking to do."

"After the ladies have gone," she agreed, giving him a quick kiss before wrapping her robe around her and struggling to her feet. She hurried to the bathroom to shower and dress, all the while blessing matchmaking butlers and mothers.

"THIS HAS BEEN LOVELY," Dorla Long said to Sam after breakfast was over and the women had gathered to say goodbye. "It's been a pleasure being in your home." She sighed and looked around the sunny dining room. "I'm going home to redecorate my house."

"I'm glad you enjoyed yourself." He edged toward the door, hoping she would follow. Those women who needed transportation were being taken by the gardener to the train station in town. The rest were getting in their rental cars and heading off for more travel agent adventures. He wished they'd hurry up and leave. He had some thinking to do, and he couldn't think while he was acting like a lord.

He couldn't believe he'd pulled it off, but the women had accepted him as Elizabeth's husband. And Elizabeth had accepted him as her lover.

Which still amazed him. Sam watched her pose by the fireplace. She'd asked him to wear his "lord" costume again, so the women could take pictures. It was worth squeezing into the tight jacket in order to see Elizabeth in one of those low-cut dresses again.

"Sam?" Elizabeth waved to him. "Would you come over here for one more picture?"

"Sure." He hid his sigh and walked across the room to stand beside her. In a few minutes it would all be over and he would be plain old Sam Martin again. He wondered if plain old Sam Martin would be enough for the lady. Sam took her hand and touched his lips to hers.

"Sam—"

"Perfect!" Barbara cried, and the flashbulbs exploded once again. He smiled down into her eyes and watched her blush.

"Lord Longford!" Sam looked up to see Ruckles standing in the doorway. The old man was clearly agitated.

"Yes, Ruckles?"

"I mean, Lady Elizabeth!" he called over the ladies' conversation. "Please, I need to see you in—"

A tall, elegant man pushed past Ruckles and entered the dining room. His smile was artificial, his clothes looked expensive, his blond hair perfectly styled. "Elizabeth, darling!"

Sam looked at her. She'd gone white, but she tried to smile. "Anthony. What a surprise!"

"A surprise, darling? I thought you were expecting me," he said, bowing to the women who had become silent.

"Several days ago," she said, finally moving from the fireplace to greet him, accepting his kiss on her cheek.

Sam caught up with them and held out his hand. "Longford. How nice to see you again."

The man's eyebrows rose as he took Sam's hand. "Yes. Same here, old man." He turned to Lizzie and lowered his voice. "Have I made a muddle of things?"

"Not if you keep your mouth shut," Sam said, wishing he could toss the man out the door. "You owe her that."

Elizabeth took Anthony's arm. "You should meet our guests before they leave. Ladies, this is my cousin, Lord...Anthony Longford."

"Oooh," one said. "Another Lord Longford. How wonderful." She shook his hand.

"Another?" Anthony repeated, turning to look at Sam.

Sam clapped him on the shoulder and spoke so only the Englishman could hear him. "Another. I'm her husband as far as they're concerned, got it?"

Anthony caught on quickly. He chatted to each woman, explained that he had expected to arrive before now, but he had been called to Tunisia on assignment for the BBC. The women, clearly charmed with his stories, followed him into the marble foyer.

Sam was ready to drown the man in the fish pond.

"MADAM, YOU ARE NEEDED downstairs immediately!"

Betsy turned to see Ruckles panting in the doorway. "You will never believe what I discovered this morning, Ruckles." She scurried over to her papers and picked up a journal from the pile of books on the bed. "I found it!"

"You have found *what*, madam?"

"The connection. The reason this room is haunted. One of your earls was a very frugal man." She waved the journal in the air. "Do you want to know what he did?"

The butler deliberately looked away. "Madam, not now. You must come with me."

"What do you mean 'not now'?" His expression didn't change, which frightened her. "Is something wrong with Sam? For heaven's sake, Ruckles, what's going on?"

"Not Mr. Sam. Lord Longford has arrived."

"What are you talking about?"

"Anthony. The ex-husband."

"The *real* one?" Betsy tossed the journal onto the bed. Shoot. What on earth could she do with a second lord? And here Sam had been doing so well. Getting Elizabeth and him together had been almost ridiculously easy. "Are you sure?"

He nodded.

"What's he doing here?"

"He did not inform me."

"Hell and damnation, the timing couldn't be worse."

The butler wrung his hands. "I am aware of that fact, madam. What should I do?"

"Stick him in the library until the guests have left."

"It is too late for that. I tried to divert him, but he was quite insistent on going into the dining room to see everyone. Lord Anthony is accustomed to having his own way."

Betsy drew herself to her full height of five feet one inch. "I will take care of that young man," she swore. "He is not going to spoil everything now, not when my destiny has finally come true."

"It's not only your destiny, madam. If Lady E. can't make a go of this, she'll have to leave Longley and so will I. And a Ruckles has never left Longley."

"Never?"

"Only when we die, madam, and then we are buried on the grounds."

Betsy followed him out the door. "Don't worry, Ruckles," she said, scurrying to keep up with his long strides. "I won't let anyone keep you out of your grave."

"WHY ARE YOU WEARING that outfit?" Anthony glanced at her bosom. "It's quite revealing for a Sunday morning."

"It's part of my English country weekend." Elizabeth took a step backward. "The one you promised to attend, remember?"

"I apologize. My secretary should have called you." He nodded toward Sam, who had been cornered by the two women from New York. "It appears you found a substitute easily enough." He chuckled. "An American. Really, Elizabeth, how did you manage it?"

"He's a good man. We had a lovely weekend." She lifted her chin and defied him to make a negative comment.

Anthony raised one eyebrow. "Defensive, are we? Do I sense a romance?"

"Don't tease."

"Ah, a romance, then. With the burly American

who keeps looking at me as if he would like to ban me from the premises."

"He probably would. He didn't want to impersonate you, but he has done an excellent job."

Anthony smiled and looked around the room. "I'm so easily replaced. Where is Ruckles? I definitely need a Bloody Mary."

"He's over there by the stairs, with Sam's mother. Oh, good, she's feeling better." Betsy Martin, dressed in a lavender pantsuit, took Sam's arm and whispered something to him while Ruckles began to carry luggage to the front door.

"What did you say her name was?"

"Betsy Martin."

"She looks familiar," he murmured as Sam and Betsy approached.

"I can't imagine why."

"Who is she?"

"A sweet lady who fell ill on a bus tour and ended up staying for the weekend. I'm so glad she's well enough to come downstairs and say goodbye to everyone."

"A bus tour? Is Dianne still trekking through here?"

Elizabeth ignored the question, especially since they both remembered an afternoon when Anthony and the tour guide had been discovered together in a linen closet. Neither one had shown the least bit of remorse. "Betsy, I'd like you to meet my cousin Anthony."

"Anthony," the older woman said, taking his hand and leaning close. "I hope you aren't messing everything up for Elizabeth."

"I'm doing my best to behave," he promised. "I think I know you."

"You do?"

"I interviewed you a few years back in Cannes. You wrote the book that the movie *Night Lover* was based upon, I believe, and it won an award."

"It won *two* awards," Betsy said. "Isn't Cannes a lovely city?"

Anthony turned to Elizabeth. "You didn't know that Mrs. Martin is a famous author?"

Elizabeth looked at Betsy, who didn't appear to be the least bit disconcerted by Anthony's pronouncement. "You are?"

The woman shrugged. "I've retired. From now on I'm going to have adventures of my own."

Elizabeth glanced at Sam, who shrugged, as well. One of the guests, overhearing the conversation, asked Betsy, "What kind of books did you write?"

Anthony answered for her. "She's the master of ghost stories, haunted houses, time travel and romance. Three of her books have been made into films and—"

"Four," Betsy said, correcting him. "Spielberg is producing one next year."

"Ghost stories," Elizabeth repeated, realizing that finally everything made sense. "I see. And you thought you found another one here?"

"Maybe a little one," Betsy said. "But completely by accident. You mustn't think I came here on purpose."

"That's exactly what I do think," Elizabeth murmured, glancing toward Sam. He stepped closer and took her hand.

"It wasn't like that," he said, keeping his voice low. "I told you, my mother has a way of creating chaos."

She removed her hand from his. "And you know how to take advantage of it. Did you stage her accident so I would let her stay? You knew I didn't want Longley to become famous for ghosts. It's ridiculous."

Betsy raised her voice. "Ruckles is going to write the story himself. He needs a little more action, of course, but I'll help him with that."

Several ladies wanted autographs, even more had read Betsy's books, and the excited voiced echoed across the marble foyer until Ruckles announced the bags were removed and waiting outside. Pattie and Peggie stood by the stairs and waited for further instructions.

"One more thing," Betsy said. "Don't you want to know why the room is haunted?"

And of course they all did.

"Follow me," she said, leading them toward the stairs. Elizabeth had no choice but to go along to the blue bedroom and plaster a smile on her face. She wanted the Martins to leave. Betsy could take her ghost stories and her handsome son and remove herself from Longley immediately after the rest of the guests left. And Anthony could follow them down the drive.

"Here," Betsy said, lifting part of the satin cover to expose one of the bed's legs. "See the initials 'HC'?"

Everyone but Elizabeth and Sam peered forward to see.

"That stands for 'Hampton Court'. Your fifth earl was lord chamberlain of the household in the Stuart court, after Queen Elizabeth."

"And?" Anthony prompted.

"Any unwanted furniture in the royal households was given to him to get rid of. I guess they did a lot of redecorating in those days, too. And the earl used a lot of it to furnish his own houses, which was perfectly legal." She straightened and dropped the satin back in place.

"Hampton Court. So this actually could have been Queen Elizabeth's bed. It *is* haunted."

"It is *not* haunted," Elizabeth insisted. "That's a very nice story, but—"

Betsy shook her head. "Don't you feel it?"

"No."

Betsy sniffed the air. "Marjoram," she said.

Ruckles nodded. "The queen used it in her favorite perfume."

"Stand over there," Betsy insisted, leading Elizabeth to the portrait. She motioned to Sam. "You, too, dear. Stand here with Lady E. and see how you feel when you look at the painting."

"I really don't—" Elizabeth stood in front of the painting, her back to her guests. She couldn't make a scene with ten travel agents watching.

Betsy backed off and murmured something to the others, but Elizabeth didn't hear. She was aware that Sam's arm was touching hers. "Get away from me," she whispered, pretending to gaze at the redheaded queen. It wasn't the most flattering painting.

"No. Not until you tell me what's wrong."

She kept her voice low. "I want you and your mother out of here. Anthony will give you a ride anywhere you need to go."

"Fine. If that's what the lady wants, that's what the lady gets."

"That's precisely what I want," she said. "So make your mother stop researching her next bestseller and let me say goodbye to my guests."

She waited as he walked away, then composed herself. She wanted to look cheerful when she turned around.

"Lizzie?"

"What?" She turned to see Sam standing by the closed door. The room was empty except for the two of them.

"The door is locked."

"Then unlock it."

"Obviously I would if I could," he said, frowning at her.

"Where did everyone go?" Elizabeth walked across the room and tried the doorknob herself. "Is this some kind of joke?"

"Maybe not a joke," he said, shrugging out of his tightly fitted coat. "And my guess is that everyone has followed my mother down the stairs."

"Ruckles wouldn't lock us in here."

"No? Not even if my mother told him he could have more time to write? She's matchmaking again."

"Well, in that case, maybe Ruckles would go along with such an idea." Elizabeth sat on the edge of the bed. "You mother has a way of convincing people to do some very odd things."

"My mother is an amazing woman. My father died when I was ten, and she managed his construction business by day and wrote books at night to make enough money to support us. I think she convinced herself that she could be rich and famous, and that's what happened."

"You lied to me."

He sat down next to her. "About what?"

"What you were doing here at Longley."

"No, I didn't." Sam took her hand. "It was just a tour on a bus, sweetheart."

She turned to face him. "Until your mother thought this room was haunted. Until she decided to research her next book, perhaps? Until the two of you thought you'd fool the little Englishwoman?"

"That's not how it happened and you know it."

"Your mother told everyone you were my husband."

He smiled and brought her hand to his lips. "Would that be such a terrible thing?"

She actually thought her heart stopped for a moment. "I couldn't leave Longley."

"I don't expect you to. We could figure something out," he promised. "If you loved me."

Elizabeth shook her head. "That's not the way it works."

"Of course it is. I love you. You love me." He placed a brief kiss on her lips. "Together we should be able to figure out how to make Longley profitable."

"*We?*"

"Yes. I wouldn't mind the challenge. We'll redo

the West Wing for my mother. I can sell my business and have enough money to rebuild Longley and satisfy the trustees." He smiled. "That is, if you can stand to be plain old Mrs. Martin for the rest of your life."

Elizabeth wrapped her arms around his neck. "I think I would like that very much."

"Good." He tipped her back onto the pillows and followed her down. "Now we finally get to make love in a bed."

"And not just any bed," she said unbuttoning his shirt. "Do you think the queen will mind?"

"I don't know," he murmured, lowering Elizabeth's lace-trimmed bodice. "If she shows up later we'll ask her."

BETSY STOOD IN THE FOYER and watched as Ruckles closed the door behind Lord Anthony. The young man had been encouraged to return to London and leave Lady Elizabeth and her new fiancé to themselves.

Ruckles glanced up the stairs. "It's very quiet up there, madam. Should I check on them?"

"No, let them fight it out." Though she knew they wouldn't fight long. She'd seen that dear girl's face when she thought she'd been duped. Sam, good, honest Sam, would convince Elizabeth that none of that was true. "Come on, Ruckles, you can lead me to a telephone. I have some calls to make."

"Yes, madam." He swept through the foyer and down a hall that led to a set of offices. "You may make yourself comfortable in here."

"Thanks, Ruckles. How are you coming with chapter four?"

"Excellent. I have added conflict and just a hint of romance."

"Wonderful. I'm glad you've changed to fiction. It's so much more exciting."

"The 'sexual tension' is still a problem," he muttered.

"It takes practice," she assured him, dialing her sister's number. Mary answered on the second ring. "Mary, you've got to rent a wheelchair and come to England. I've met my destiny, and Sam is marrying a lovely young woman. Yes, *really.* And by the way, Queen Elizabeth says hello."

Take 4 bestselling love stories FREE

Plus get a FREE surprise gift!

Special Limited-time Offer

Mail to Harlequin Reader Service®

3010 Walden Avenue
P.O. Box 1867
Buffalo, N.Y. 14240-1867

YES! Please send me 4 free Harlequin Love and Laughter™ novels and my free surprise gift. Then send me 4 brand-new novels every other month, which I will receive months before they appear in bookstores. Bill me at the low price of $2.90 each plus 25¢ delivery per book and applicable sales tax if any*. That's the complete price and a savings of over 10% off the cover prices—quite a bargain! I understand that accepting the books and gift places me under no obligation ever to buy any books. I can always return a shipment and cancel at any time. Even if I never buy another book from Harlequin, the 4 free books and the surprise gift are mine to keep forever.

102 BPA A7EF

Name	(PLEASE PRINT)	
Address	Apt. No.	
City	State	Zip

This offer is limited to one order per household and not valid to present Love and Laughter™ subscribers. *Terms and prices are subject to change without notice. Sales tax applicable in N.Y.

ULL-397   ©1996 Harlequin Enterprises Limited

LOVE & LAUGHTER LET'S CELEBRATE SWEEPSTAKES
OFFICIAL RULES—NO PURCHASE NECESSARY

To enter, complete an Official Entry Form or 3" x 5" card by hand printing the words "Love & Laughter Let's Celebrate Sweepstakes," your name and address thereon and mailing it to: in the U.S., Love & Laughter Let's Celebrate Sweepstakes, P.O. Box 9076, Buffalo, NY 14269-9076, or in Canada to, Love & Laughter Let's Celebrate Sweepstakes, P.O. Box 637, Fort Erie, Ontario L2A 5X3. Limit: one entry per envelope, one prize to an individual, family or organization. Entries must be sent via first-class mail and be received no later than 11/30/97. No liability is assumed for lost, late, misdirected or nondelivered mail.

Three (3) winners will be selected in a random drawing (to be conducted no later than 12/31/97) from among all eligible entries received by D. L. Blair, Inc., an independent judging organization whose decisions are final, to each receive a collection of 15 Love & Laughter Romantic Comedy videos (approximate retail value: $250 U.S. per collection).

Sweepstakes offer is open only to residents of the U.S. (except Puerto Rico) and Canada who are 18 years of age or older, except employees and immediate family members of Harelquin Enterprises, Ltd., their affiliates, subsidiaries, and all other agencies, entities and persons connected with the use, marketing or conduct of this sweepstakes. All applicable laws and regulations apply. Offer void wherever prohibited by law. Taxes and/or duties on prizes are the sole responsibility of the winners. Any litigation within the province of Quebec respecting the conduct and awarding of prize may be submitted to the Régie des alcools, des courses et des jeux. All prizes will be awarded; winners will be notified by mail. No substitution for prizes is permitted. Odds of winning are dependent upon the number of eligible entries received.

Any prize or prize notification returned as undeliverable may result in the awarding of that prize to an alternative winner. By acceptance of their prize, winners consent to use of their names, photographs or likenesses for purposes of advertising, trade and promotion on behalf of Harlequin Enterprises, Ltd., without further compensation unless prohibited by law. In order to win a prize, residents of Canada will be required to correctly answer a time-limited, arithmetical skill-testing question administered by mail.

For a list of winners (available after December 31, 1997), send a separate stamped, self-addressed envelope to: Love & Laughter Let's Celebrate Sweepstakes Winner, P.O. Box 4200, Blair, NE 68009-4200, U.S.A.

LLRULES

As Seen on TV!

Free Gift Offer

With a Free Gift proof-of-purchase
from any Harlequin® book, you can receive
a beautiful cubic zirconia pendant.

This stunning marquise-shaped stone is a genuine cubic
zirconia—accented by an 18" gold tone necklace.
(Approximate retail value $19.95)

Send for yours today...
compliments of ◈HARLEQUIN®

To receive your free gift, a cubic zirconia pendant, send us one original proof-of-purchase, photocopies not accepted, from the back of any Harlequin Romance®, Harlequin Presents®, Harlequin Temptation®, Harlequin Superromance®, Harlequin Intrigue®, Harlequin American Romance®, or Harlequin Historicals® title available at your favorite retail outlet, together with the Free Gift Certificate, plus a check or money order for $1.65 U.S./$2.15 CAN. (do not send cash) to cover postage and handling, payable to Harlequin Free Gift Offer. We will send you the specified gift. Allow 6 to 8 weeks for delivery. Offer good until December 31, 1997, or while quantities last. Offer valid in the U.S. and Canada only.

Free Gift Certificate

Name: _____

Address: _____

City: _____ State/Province: _____ Zip/Postal Code: _____

Mail this certificate, one proof-of-purchase and a check or money order for postage and handling to: HARLEQUIN FREE GIFT OFFER 1997. In the U.S.: 3010 Walden Avenue, P.O. Box 9071, Buffalo NY 14269-9057. In Canada: P.O. Box 604, Fort Erie, Ontario L2Z 5X3.

FREE GIFT OFFER   084-KEZ

ONE PROOF-OF-PURCHASE
To collect your fabulous FREE GIFT, a cubic zirconia pendant, you must include this
original proof-of-purchase for each gift with the properly completed Free Gift Certificate.

084-KEZR

Celebrate with

LOVE & LAUGHTER™

Love to watch movies?

Enter now to win a FREE 15-copy video collection of romantic comedies in Love & Laughter's Let's Celebrate Sweepstakes.

WIN A ROMANTIC COMEDY VIDEO COLLECTION!

To enter the Love & Laughter Let's Celebrate Sweepstakes, complete an Official Entry Form or hand print on a 3" x 5" card the words "Love & Laughter Let's Celebrate Sweepstakes," your name and address and mail to: "Love & Laughter Let's Celebrate Sweepstakes," in the U.S., 3010 Walden Avenue, P.O. Box 9076, Buffalo, N.Y. 14269-9076; in Canada, P.O. Box 637, Fort Erie, Ontario L2A 5X3. Limit: one entry per envelope, one prize to an individual family or organization. Entries must be sent via first-class mail and be received no later than November 30, 1997. See back page ad for complete sweepstakes rules.

Celebrate with Love & Laughter™!

Official Entry Form

"Please enter me in the Love & Laughter Let's Celebrate Sweepstakes"

Name: _____

Address: _____

City: _____

State/Prov.: _____ Zip/Postal Code: _____

LLENTRY

LLENTRY